THE GOLDEN WINDLASS

Sequel to the Stowaway

Mike Simmons

Paper Girders publishing
Tel: 07932907653
Email papergirders@gmail.com
Web: wwwpapergirderspublishing.com
Cover design and illustrations by Alan Padwick
Proof Reading and Editing by Fran Thorne
ISBN 979 8 6442605 9 1

British Library Cataloguing in Publication Data. A catalogue record for this book is available from the British Library.

Dedicated to the memory of Melena Elizabeth Simmons.

CONTENTS

CHAPTER ONE

Zed's friend Dwain

Zed looked out from the window of his classroom on the second floor of his comprehensive school in South London. It was raining and cold. Two fire engines, their blue lights reflecting off the wet pavements, weaved in and out of the heavy traffic on the main road leading to the Rotherhithe Tunnel. Over the shiny roofs of the houses he could just see the top of Tower Bridge.

Below in the school car park Mr Pinhead, the caretaker, was pushing a big trolley loaded with metal chairs. Holding a large umbrella in his left hand, and pushing the trolley with the other, he would occasionally veer out of control nearly colliding with the parked cars. His real name was Mr Pine, but they called him 'Pinhead' because of his pointed head and sharp tongue. They were always teasing him, and he was always shouting at them, and complaining to the head teacher about them. Zed hoped that he would crash into the cars, then he would be in trouble.

He was now in Year Nine and had worked hard in the last two years. His reading and writing had greatly improved and, apart from one small mishap in January when he and another boy got into trouble for throwing snowballs at Pinhead. Zed was normally attentive in lessons, but today was different. It was the last lesson of the last day of term, and like all the other children he couldn't wait to get out for the two weeks holiday.

He was going to spend the Easter holidays with Peggy, Tim and Barney the collie, in the cottage on the canal. He hadn't seen them since last summer, and It had now been two years since Peggy had discovered him stowing away on the narrowboat Kingfisher which she was taking to Boswell's Yard. He had run away from the circus, where he was living with his horrible Uncle Darren after his mum Amanda had been sent to prison and he had been excluded from his junior school.

A large black crow landed on the branch of a tree opposite the classroom window. 'Hello crow,' mouthed Zed, pressing his lips to the glass. The crow opened its beak wide, cawed, and cocked its head to one side.

2

'At least yer free,' mouthed Zed. The bird spread its wings and flew off towards another tree. A shrill voice called from the front of the classroom.

'Zed Hawkins, what are you doing?'

Talking to a crow Miss.' The class all laughed. The teacher smiled. 'Do you often talk to birds, Zed?

'No Miss, but 'e was talking to me.'

I know it's the last day of term, Zed, but I would rather you paid attention to me than to a crow.

Zed nodded. Yes, Miss.

The school bell rang at dead on three thirty in the afternoon.

'Wait, not yet,'' cried Miss Swan, as her pupils rushed towards the exit.

'Have a lovely Easter, everybody,'' she said, opening the door. As Zed passed by, she touched him on the shoulder.

'Any adventures this holiday Zed?''

'I'm going to stay on the canals again Miss, with Tim and Peggy.''

'Miss Swan smiled. ''I look forward to hearing all about it, when we come back'

See yer Miss,'' said Zed, as he ran down the corridor to catch up with his friend Dwain. He had met Dwain through his friend Kevin who he had known since junior school. They all lived on the same housing estate in Rotherhithe.

Walking home, the rain turned to sleet.

'I 'ope it snows,'' said Dwain.

'I don't,' replied Zed, 'I might not be able to get to Tim and Peggy's.'

Dwain asked when he was going.

'Sunday morning, gonna meet Peggy at Paddington Station.'

'You lucky git.' said Dwain, 'wish I could get out

3

of this dump for Easter.'

Zed thought for a moment. 'Would yer mum let you come?' he asked.

'Spec' so. She'd be glad to get rid of me.'

'Peggy'll ring tonight, I could ask 'er if you could come too, if yer like.'

Dwain, punched Zed on the arm. 'That'll be cool man, ain't never stayed on a boat before.'

'We don't stay on the boats,' said Zed, 'we stay in Tim's cottage, though we'll probably go out on the boats.'

Dwain lived with his mum, elder sister and his one-eyed cat, Eric, on the fourth floor of a block of flats called Trafalgar House. Dwain's mum had adopted Eric after Kevin's family moved to North London, where they weren't allowed pets. The vet had removed Eric's eye after someone had shot him with an airgun. Dwain never mentioned his dad, so Zed never asked about him. Dwain was the same age as Zed, though he was taller with thick black hair. There was a small scar above his eye where his sister had thrown a glass ashtray at him when they were smaller. Zed always envied Dwain's thick black hair and dark skin, he hated being ginger and having freckles. In the summer, Gran was always nagging him about wearing sun cream and a hat.

'There's another reason why I want to get out of 'ere,' said Dwain suddenly.

'What's that?' asked Zed.

'Mum's just found out my sister's pregnant.'

Zed was shocked. 'What? I thought she was only...?'

Yeah Sixteen,' replied Dwain. 'So, there's a load of stuff going down now.

'What's she gonna do?' asked Zed.

Dwain shook his head. 'Dunno. She wants to keep it, but me mums said she's gotta get rid of it.'

'That's bad man,'' replied Zed.

4

Old Dewey, the lollipop man, was standing on the kerb when they reached the crossing that led to the busy main road. They all called him Dewey because he always had a dew drop hanging from his long nose, even in the summer.

'Wait there,' he said to Zed and Dwain in a loud gruff tone.

Wearing a long yellow coat and peaked cap, he shuffled slowly into the middle of the road before holding his lollipop stick up high, bringing the traffic to a sudden halt. Dewey glared at the driver of a black BMW as it screeched to a halt close to his feet, loud rap music blaring from the open windows.

Dewey shouted above the noise, 'right, over you go.'

'Thanks Dewey,'' shouted Zed, as they ran to the other side of the road.

'I heard that, you little scruff.' called Dewey, shuffling to the opposite kerb.

Zed and Dwain reached the pub called the George which was on the corner of the road which led to the entrance to the housing estate where they both lived. The estate that Trafalgar and Nelson blocks was on wasn't as big as some housing estates in London. There were four high rise blocks with ten floors in each block. Built in the 1960s, in dull grey concrete, all the buildings seemed to merge into one huge blob of concrete. Each block had its own car park. There was a green open space in the middle of the estate, and what remained of a once well used children's playground.

'Laters'. said Zed when they reached the entrance to Trafalgar House. Text yer when I 've spoken to Peggy.'

Dwain pressed the keypad on the blue steel door. 'Laters,' he called, then took the lift to the fourth floor. When Zed reached the entrance to Nelson House a group of older teenagers was hanging around outside the door. Since he returned home two years ago, they had been pestering him to join their 'crew', even though he was only eleven at the time. They said he could be a 'runner', whatever that was. Gran had told him to stay away from them, as she thought they were involved with drugs.

'Hey Zed man, what's 'appening?' called Bradley Seaton who lived on the floor below Zed. He was fifteen and always in trouble. Gran said that he went to a pupil referral unit because he had been expelled from two schools.

'Got any dosh' man?' asked Bradley.

'No,' said Zed, firmly.

Bradley Seaton pulled his hood down further over his face. 'Come on man, you must 'ave some on yer. I bet yer gran keeps some dosh in the flat,'

'I don't rob off no-one, let alone me gran,' said Zed.

'Not like yer uncle then?' replied Bradley.

Zed punched in the code to unlock the steel door. 'No, I'm not, and I don't wanna be either,'

Another hooded youth blocked his way. Ow's yer old woman then, still banged up?'

'Get out my way,' said Zed, pushing the door open.

Zed could hear them laughing as he stepped into the lift. It moved slowly up to the eighth floor, rocking gently from side to side. How he hated this place, he couldn't wait to get away. When he got home, he told Gran about the conversation with Dwain, and said that he was going to ask Peggy if his friend could go with him.

When Peggy rang that evening, Zed raced to pick up the phone.

'See next week, Peg, me mate Dwain, right,

well 'is sister's pregnant and 'is mum 'as said she's gotta get rid of it, and 'e ain't got a dad and.........
Peggy shouted. 'Zed, stop. 'Good grief boy, are you asking me if Dwain can come with you next week?'

'Oh could 'e, Peg? 'E'd really luv it.'
 After he had calmed down, she asked if his mum would let him come?'

'She wants to get rid of 'im,' said Zed, 'e told me.'
 Peggy laughed. 'I'm sure she didn't mean it like that, the poor woman must have enough on her plate with the sister.'

'Gran knows 'is mum,' said Zed, she could phone 'er tonight.'

'Alright,' said Peg, 'but I'll have to ask Tim first. Now let me have another word
with your gran.'

'Bye, Peggy,' called Zed, as Gran took the phone from his hand.

'I meant to ask you earlier, how's Amanda?' asked Peggy.

'Not too long now and she'll be out of prison.' said Gran.

 Amanda, Zed's mum, was in the last three months of a prison sentence and had been moved from a closed prison in North London to an open prison in Kent near the South coast. Zed thought this was funny, and asked Gran why, if there was no wall, she couldn't just walk out and come home. Amanda was insistent that she didn't want Zed to visit her in prison, so he and Gran used to speak to her on the phone every week. Zed would tell her all about how well he was doing at school, and his forthcoming Easter visit to Tim and Peggy's. She would tell him that she felt a lot better now, and didn't need to take that nasty stuff anymore. Gran was also pleased that Amanda had passed some exams whilst in prison, and was attending textiles classes, which would help her to get a job when she was released. Peggy wanted to do all she could to help Amanda in the future, and knew how much Zed loved and missed his mum.

Tim and his friend Rocket Ron had spent the last few days working in the dry dock at Boswell's Yard. The steel hulls, or bottoms, of the narrowboats Odin and Thor, had been cleaned off using a high-pressure hose, then after being inspected for any pitting or rusting, a new coat of black bitumen had been brushed on. They would not need to be blacked again for another three years. Now with the job complete, they could be moved back to their mooring by Tim's cottage next to the lock on the canal.

Tim had lived here since he was a child. His father had been the lockkeeper and had been responsible for maintaining all the locks between the village of Tiddledurn and Melbury, five miles away. Tim had bought the cottage from British Waterways after his dad had died. He had learned a lot of skills from his father and had become a very good mechanic and engineer.

Both Odin and Thor were seventy foot in Length. Odin had an engine, Thor was called a butty and didn't have an engine, but was moved along the canal by either being towed astern, or tied alongside 'Odin'. Each boat had 12 bunk beds, toilets, or 'heads' which Tim called 'bucket and chuck it' a kitchen or 'galley' with folding tables and benches, and a wonderful wood burning stove. At the stern, or back of the boat, there were small skipper's cabins -one for Tim and one for Peggy, where they stayed when they were on board. Each boat had a wooden frame supporting a canvas roof which could be rolled back in the summer. This was great fun for the groups staying on the boats, as they could lay on their bunks and sunbathe as they moved along.

8

It was getting dark. Tim and Rocket Ron were cold, wet and hungry. Barney, Tim's collie was bored. Tim pushed open the small wooden door that led from the dry dock. They both shivered as the cold wind chased them across the car park to where Tim had parked his old Series One Land Rover, which he affectionally called Betsy. He had agreed to call on Peggy once he had dropped Rocket Ron home.

Peggy had made all the arrangements for Zed's visit on Sunday, but there was no point in getting there before EastEnders had finished, so he called into the Black Horse pub for a pint, and maybe a game of pool if there was time.

Using the spare door key Tim let himself into Peggy's small flat above Strout's' butcher's shop. She had lived here in the village of Tiddledurn for two years, ever since her little narrowboat, Turtle, had gone up in flames. It was Rocket Ron who had saved Peggy. Walking his two ferrets Frankie and Freddie he saw smoke coming from the window, and after getting no response, he pushed open the door. He found Peggy slumped unconscious in the chair, and the boat full of flames and smoke. He pulled her out and called the fire brigade. The boat was destroyed along with all her belongings, and memories. She was kept in hospital overnight, and then stayed with Tim in his cottage for four weeks before moving into the flat. What remained of the boat had been taken away to be scrapped. Tim had rescued   Turtles wooden nameplate. Carefully he had repaired and varnished it, then screwed it to the wall in her flat as a reminder of her little boat that she had lost.

Every day she touched the sign and promised herself that a new Turtle would soon be afloat on the canal. Barney went dashing up the stairs, bursting into the sitting room and jumping onto the sofa. Peggy had just finished painting a Buckby can. This was a can for carrying water or milk and used by families on the old working boats. It was often decorated in the traditional way with roses and castles. Peggy had been interested in canal art since she was a girl. When she had finished, they would be sold in the canal shop by the lock.

'What time is Zed coming on Sunday?' asked Tim.

'I'm meeting him at Paddington at eleven o'clock. That's what I wanted to talk to you about. He asked if he could bring his friend Dwain.'

Tim thought for a moment. 'It's alright with me, he'll have to sleep in Zed's room though.'

'He knows that,' said Peggy.

''Fine then,'' said Tim. 'No problem, is it Barney?' Barney didn't hear, he was fast asleep on the sofa.

After Tim had left, Peggy rang Gran to let her know that Tim was fine with Dwain staying. Zed was still packing when Gran came into his room.

'Peggy just phoned and said she'd spoken to Tim, and it would be alright to take Dwain, I'll ring his mum in the morning.'

'Brill,'' said Zed. 'I'll text 'I'm.'

'But it's after ten,'' said Gran.

'E'll still be up.' Zed reached into his pocket for his phone. U CUM 2.

The reply came back quickly. YH COOLIO.

Dwain stayed with Zed on Saturday night. His mum was worried that he wouldn't get up in time. He had arrived carrying his clothes in a large plastic launderette bag.

'That's all we 'ad', said Dwain, noting Gran's surprise.

She laughed. 'Well you're certainly not travelling with that thing. We've got a

spare ruck-sack that belonged to Zed's uncle. You can put

10

your clothes in that.' Peggy rang that evening to check that everything was ok and that the boys had enough warm clothing, the Easter weather forecast was cold and wet. She told Gran that she would meet them all at Paddington Station at eleven o'clock in the morning. Gran asked about the cost of the tickets. Peggy said that she already had them, and not to worry.

The boys didn't sleep well, partly due to them being topped and tailed in Zed's single bed. Twice Dwain was woken after Zed kicked him in the face. When he told Zed in the morning, he laughed saying he must have been dreaming. They had both woken early and lay talking for some time.

'What are Tim and Peggy like?'' asked Dwain.
Zed thought for a moment.

'Tim's big and 'e's got a thick, droopy moustache, always wears a red scarf round his neck, never seen I'm without it, oh, and 'e's got very big 'ands. Peggy's really nice, always wears bright dresses, you know like flowery stuff. When I was with them last summer it was like 'aving a real mum and dad.'
Dwain asked about Barney.
Zed replied that he was a Border Collie. 'Tim got him from a rescue centre in North Wales. Barney goes everywhere with 'im, and 'e's clever, knows every word yer say.'

'Do you miss not seeing yer dad? asked Dwain.
Zed yawned. 'Dunno really, Gran says what you've never 'ad, you never miss.'

'I would've liked a proper brother to play with though.'
Dwain sat up and swung his legs onto the floor. What do yer mean a proper brother?'

'I've got a step brother called Conner,' said Zed. 'Lives with me dad, I only see 'im a couple of times a

11

year, 'e's a bit thick though.'

Dwain was quiet for a moment. 'I never see my dad.'

Zed asked why not.

'Mum said he went back to Jamaica, when I was three.

'That's really bad man,' said Zed.

They heard the radio come on in the kitchen.

'Oh no,' said Zed throwing the duvet back. 'Radio Two, Gran loves it, says she misses Terry Wogan though.

Oo's 'e?' asked Dwain.

'You know, that bloke who did the Pudsey Bear thing on the telly.'

Gran called from the kitchen. 'Come on you two, up you get, breakfast in twenty minutes.'

CHAPTER TWO

Paddington to Melbury

It was nine thirty when they left the flat for the journey by bus and underground to Paddington Station.

Gran hated going on the tube train, she was frightened that a bomb might go off, or that the train would break down in the tunnel. Zed said that if it did break down, he would get out and walk along then track, rather than miss meeting Peggy.

The station was heaving with people. Pushing though the crowds they slowly made their way to the main entrance, where Peggy was meeting them by the statue of Isambard Kingdom Brunel who had designed the station many years before.

Zed was the first to spot Peggy, not that you could really miss her. She was wearing a thick, bright yellow woollen jacket that came down to her knees and a knitted green hat with yellow daffodils on it. He ran towards her and threw himself into her arms.

'Steady on,' she shouted, giving Zed a big hug, 'you'll knock me over.'

'This is Dwain, my friend I told you about.'

Peggy shook his hand firmly. 'Hello Dwain, it's nice to meet you.'

Zed's told me lots about you and Tim.' he said.

She laughed. 'My, my, all good I hope.'

Peggy greeted Gran with a kiss on the cheek. 'Hello Betty, bet you'll be glad to get rid of him for two weeks.'

'I will indeed, replied Gran with a wink. 'I might have some food left in the cupboard now.'

'Right, come on then,' said Peggy, 'we need platform five, the train leaves in thirty minutes.'

Dwain had never been to Paddington Station

before, and could not believe the size of it, and how tall the roof was. He had never travelled on a train other than the underground. In fact, Dwain, like Zed had never really travelled anywhere far from the housing estate in Rotherhithe, South London where they had been born thirteen years ago.

'What's a buffet?' he asked Peggy pointing to the large sign on the side of one of the carriages.
She told him that its where you can buy refreshments, like tea and sandwiches, and that it's pronounced buffay.

'Must be French or summink,' said Zed.
Their carriage was a long way down the platform. Dwain had run ahead to have a look in the driver's cab.

'I've reserved seats,' said Peggy. She gave Zed the numbers and told him to go on the train and find them
He shouted to Dwain. 'Come on, you can't drive it.'

Peggy stood talking to Gran through the open window. There was a sudden slamming of doors, and whistles blowing, then a jolt as the train started to move slowly out of the station. Both boys had seats by the window and waved to Gran as it gathered speed. Their Easter adventure had started.

On Sunday morning, with Barney sitting on the passenger seat next to him, Tim drove his old land rover, Betsy, the five miles from his cottage, next to the canal, into town to meet Peggy and the boys from the train.

Melbury was a small county town, with quirky shops either side of a narrow high street. At the far end of town St Stephen's church spire towered over the market place, where every Friday farmers from all over the county would bring their cattle to be auctioned.

He passed under the bridge which carried the railway over the road, then drove the short distance up the hill to the station entrance. The platform was empty apart from a young guy sitting on a bench strumming an

14

old acoustic guitar covered in stickers.

He watched as two grey mice chased each other along the rail before disappearing down a hole in the bank. Minutes later the incoming intercity train from London pulled slowly into the station, pushing before it a great mass of cold air, that washed like a wave over the narrow platform. Tim shivered and pulled his scarf up around his face as the train shuddered to a halt.

'Barnee...' an excited voice called from the along the platform.

'Go on, go get him,' said Tim, as Barney ran, weaving in and out of the other alighting passengers, until he reached Zed.

'Allo Barney, you old collie, I've really missed you.' Barney jumped up to lick Zed's face.

'Oh Zed.' called Peggy, 'don't let him do that, he might have been licking his bum.' Zed didn't care, he was reunited with his mate.

'Hello little man.' said Tim, ruffling Zed's red hair with his large hand.
And who's this then?' he said, looking at Dwain.

'Dwain, my mate,' said Zed.
Tim laughed. 'Oh, you've got some mates, have you?'
Peggy interrupted. 'Oh, be quiet, don't you start.'

'Anyway Dwain, it's nice to meet you,' said Tim, shaking his hand. 'Come on let's get going, we'll freeze to death on this platform. You two can go in the back with the dog.'
Tim dropped the tailboard of the Land Rover and Barney and the boys jumped in. After passing through the darkened town Tim turned off the main road and onto a rough track that led to his cottage by the lock. The boys and Barney were thrown about in the back as the Land Rover slithered along in the wet mud.

'We're here,' shouted Zed, as they shuddered to a

15

halt. Tim yanked on the handbrake, Everybody out.' he called

Before leaving the cottage, Tim had lit a huge fire in the kitchen, piled high with freshly cut logs from the nearby woods.

'It's lovely and warm in here.'' said Peggy pushing open the kitchen door. 'Why don't you boys take your bags through to the bedroom?''

'Wow.' shouted Zed, as he opened the door. The spare room that he had previously slept in had been transformed. Gone was the old furniture, the chest of drawers with the cracked mirror, and the wonky bed with the hard mattress. In their place was a bunk bed, with brightly coloured duvet's, a fitted wardrobe and a new Dwain speechless. Peggy had painted a huge picture of the narrowboat 'Kingfisher', with Zed standing on the stern steering it. She told him that it was to remind them of how they had first met, when Zed had run away from his cruel uncle in the circus and stowed away on the Kingfisher. The circus still came each summer to the field at the edge of the village, where they would erect a tall white tent, known as a 'big top' and surround it with brightly coloured caravans and trailers. This is where Tim and Peggy had first seen Zed, a grubby little boy being made to sell programmes by his Uncle Darren. Peggy had thought he could do with a good meal. Since then Zed had neither seen nor heard from his uncle, and he didn't want to either. He had not been in contact with Zed's Gran, his own mother either, so nobody knew if he was still working at the circus.

'Right,' said Peggy, 'I ''ll leave you to unpack your things while I get some tea on the go.' Barney had already made himself comfortable on the bottom bunk.
Zed asked Dwain which bunk he wanted.

'You choose, it's your room.' he replied.

16

'Alright,' said Zed, 'I'll 'ave the bottom one.' He leaped on the bed, squashing Barney against the wall.

Dwain hauled himself up onto the top bunk. 'I can't believe this place, no wonder you like it 'ere.'

'You wait till yer see the boats, replied Zed, unpacking his bag into the wardrobe.

'Ave year ever driven 'em?' asked Dwain.

'Yeah, 'I steered Kingfisher, the boat I stowed away on, and now I'm older Tim lets me steer the butty, when he's towing it.''

Dwain stuffed some clothes into a drawer. 'What's a butty?' he asked.

'It's a boat without an engine,' said Zed.

There was a loud bang on the outside of the bedroom window.

'Come on you two, give me a hand with these logs, shouted Tim.

The boys ran outside. Tim loaded them up with armfuls of logs, which they carried inside and stacked next to the roaring fire to dry off.

Peggy called from the kitchen. 'Wash your hands, tea's ready.'

In the middle of the room next to the kitchen was a large oak table with four chairs. Peggy had laid four places and put a large bowl of hot vegetable soup in the middle of the table. Another plate was full of slices of fresh crusty bread.

She ladled the soup out into the dishes. 'Bon Appétit' she said, sitting down. Dwain was just about to ask what 'Bon Appétit' meant when there was a sudden crack followed by a loud shriek. Peggy's chair had collapsed underneath her and she was sprawled on the floor with her legs waving about in the air.

'You've broken my chair!' shouted Tim. 'Do you know how many years I 've had that?

17

Peggy struggled to her feet. 'You, you! she shouted, shaking her fist at Tim. 'You and your rotten old furniture. It's like everything else here, including you, riddled with woodworm.'

'That's an antique''

'Antique my-------'she suddenly remembered that Zed and Dwain were sitting there.

'You alright, Peggy? asked Zed barely able to stop himself from laughing.

'Yes, apart from a sore bum.'

'Do you want me to rub some ointment on it?' asked Tim, laughing.

Peggy carefully eased herself into another chair. 'Oh, do shut up.'

The boys burst into laughter.

'Are they always like this?' Dwain whispered to Zed.

He grinned. 'Yeah, always, and they're not even married.'

After they had finished the soup, they sat around the fire toasting muffins. Barney was curled up on an old blanket by the side of Tim's chair. He told them how both the boats, Odin and Thor, were in dry dock at Boswell's Yard having had their bottoms blacked. Dwain laughed at this. Tim said that he and Rocket Ron would be going back tomorrow to tidy round and re flood the dry dock.

'I really wanted to take the boats down to Boswell's in January,'' he said, 'but we were iced in.'

'Why do they call 'im Rocket Ron?' asked Zed.

Tim laughed. 'He was on his boat one day, and his gas bottle exploded. The force was so great that it blew him out of the door, just like a rocket.'

'Blimey he was lucky!'

Tim nodded. 'He was Zed, very lucky. The boat was a right off though.'

'Where's 'e live now then?'

'He's back on a boat. Can't imagine Ron living anywhere else,' added Peggy.

Dwain asked Tim what a dry dock was. Tim explained that it was just like the lock outside. 'You fill the dock with water, drive the boat in, then pump the water out leaving the dock dry. The boat rests on wooden beams, then you can work on the hull in the dry.'

'The hull's the bottom of the boat,' added Zed.

Zed pushed another muffin onto the stick. 'We could come with you tomorrow Tim.'

He shook his head. 'No, not on your first day. You take Dwain out and show him around, you'll have plenty of time on the boats, when we bring them back from Boswells Yard.'

'Great,' said Zed.

'Will we sleep on the boats?' asked Dwain.

'You will,' said Tim. 'It will take two days, so we'll have to sleep over one night. Zed can show you all he's learned since he's been coming here.'

Dwain asked Tim if it was true that there were ghosts on the canal, or was Zed making it up.

Tim smiled. 'On no, 'there are ghosts alright, and ....' He was just about to
say something else when Peggy interrupted him.

'I think it's time you two got some shut eye, don't you?'

Sleep came quickly that night. They lay talking for a short time but the soothing sound of water leaking through the top lock gates and the darkness of the room soon sent them off into a world of dreams. Peggy peeped into the room before she went to bed. A shaft of light from the open door fell upon the bunk beds. Both boys were buried deep beneath the heavy duvets that she had put on each bed. She closed the door and smiled. 'Goodnight my little Stowaway.'

19

CHAPTER THREE

Different to London

By the time the boys awoke the next morning, Tim and Barney had long since left to pick up Rocket Ron and go to the dry dock at Boswell's Yard. Ron was older than Tim and preferred the term 'rotund' rather than 'fat' when describing his physique. He had worked as a 'cooper' making wooden barrels at the Melbury Brewery but retired after suffering a mild heart attack.

'So, what are you two going to do with yourselves today?' asked Peggy over a breakfast of bacon and eggs. And before they had time to answer she added,

'You wrap up well now, it's a cold wind out there.'

'I thought we'd go and see 'arry at the marina,' said Zed.

'It's Harry, love,' said Peggy.

'It has an H at the front of it.'

Zed was getting used to Peggy and Tim correcting his speech.

'Sorry,' he said, "I meant Harry.'

Peggy said she was going to Melbury town to do some shopping and that the boys must be back by six o'clock. Checking that Zed had his mobile she gave him a spare door key. The weak April sun disguised the cold air outside. Pulling their hoods up tightly over their heads Zed thought how different it was to last summer when he had spent nearly the whole time in shorts and a tee-shirt. As they reached the lock Dwain stopped and jumped up onto the painted white end of the long wooden gate to tie up the laces in his trainers.

'That's called a balance beam,' said Zed.

'What is?' asked Dwain.

'That thing you're sitting on. You push that to open the lock gate.'

Dwain jumped down and tried pushing it. 'It won't budge.'

Zed laughed. 'That's because there's no water in the lock, I'll show you 'ow it works.' He walked along the bank so he was standing the same distance from each gate.

'Right,' he said, pointing to the bottom gates. 'Imagine there's a boat coming into the lock, you would open one of them fully to let the boat in, then close it. Now the boat is sitting down there, between the top and bottom gates, that's called the chamber.'

'Don't people fall in and drown?' Dwain asked Zed.

'Sometimes. But Tim says it's often because they haven't been taught 'ow to do it properly.'

Standing by the top gate, next to the balance beam that Dwain had been sitting on, Zed pointed to a white metal post on the side of the concrete ledge.

'These are called ground paddles, you put yer windlass on this spindle and wind 'em up. When you've opened both the ground paddles, the water gushes in from the canal and fills the lock, and the boat floats up with it. Then, when the water level in the lock is the same as the canal, you can push the gate open and drive out.'

'Wow,' said Dwain, 'that's brill man.' Though he thought it sounded a bit confusing.

You'll get used to it.' said Zed.

As the boys ran down the grass bank alongside the bottom gates, they saw Sammy and Sheena, Tim's two adopted swans, having an early morning wash in the canal. Zed told Dwain that when Sammy was a cygnet, a young swan, he had a fishing hook lodged in his mouth, Tim had caught him and removed it. Since then he's never left. Then two years ago, along came Sheena and they've been together ever since.

Ow do you tell the boy from the girl? asked Dwain.

Zed said he couldn't remember. 'Tim did tell me once, it's something to do with their beak.

'Don't think I'd like to try and catch one, said Dwain.

'Nor me,' laughed Zed. 'They reckon their wing can break yer arm.'

It was only a mile along the towpath to Harry Martin's marina. Zed showed Dwain where he and Simon had camped last summer, and told him about the tent that Tim and Peggy had bought him,

'You'd like Simon. He comes from Ghana and now lives over 'ere in England.

Dwain asked how they had met.

'E was one of the kids in a group we took on the camper boats last year. We got on well so I asked Tim and Peg if 'e could come and stay.'

22

They passed the spot where Army Jim was moored, and the field where the little donkey always came to the gate for a carrot.

'Why do they call 'im that?' asked Dwain.

Zed shrugged. 'That's what Tim calls 'im, cos 'e always dresses in army gear, and carries a long knife strapped to 'is leg. Dunno where 'e is now though.' Zed had always been a bit scared of Army Jim. The footpath was wet and muddy underfoot and in some places the puddles were so wide they had to almost climb into the hedge to get along.

An abandoned fibre glass made cruiser was bobbing up and down alongside the bank. The inside was flooded, and old bits of furniture were floating in the water. Dwain jumped onto the stern of the boat and started playing with the steering wheel, while Zed stood on the gunwales at the side of the boat, rocking it to and fro, shouting 'rough seas ahead, hold tight everyone.' Suddenly the line securing the stern end to the bank snapped. Zed just managed to jump off onto the towpath.

'Ah! Zed! Help me!' shrieked Dwain, as the stern of the boat started to drift across the canal.

Zed just laughed. 'You said you wanted to go on a boat, didn't you? Shall I let
the front line go, too?'

'No! No! don't!' screamed Dwain. 'It might turn over and sink! '

'Throw me the line then, and I can pull you in.' shouted Zed still laughing.

Dwain grabbed what was left of the stern line and threw it towards Zed. It went up in the air, landing in the canal.

'What was that? You're supposed to coil it first.' called Zed.

Dwain leant over the side to grab the line from the water.

'Catch it then.' he shouted to Zed, who was still in fits of laughter.

'I can't catch it if it doesn't reach me, can I? Coil it up, don't just chuck it.'

After three more attempts Zed managed to catch the line and secure it to a metal ring in the bank. Dwain was just pleased to be back on dry ground.

'You sure yer still up for this boating stuff Dwain? said Zed.

'Very funny. I could've drowned.'

'Don't you say anything to Tim and Peggy about this when we get 'ome. They won't be 'appy if they know we've been playing about on a boat without a buoyancy aid on.'

'Course I won't.' replied Dwain. 'What's a buoyancy aid?'

Zed explained that its a jacket that keeps you afloat if you fall in water.

'We have to wear 'em all the time when we're on the boats.'

A narrow bridge hole from the canal led into Harry Martin's marina. Harry's was a small marina compared to some, but well used by local and passing boaters alike. They would come in for fuel, coal and gas, or to fill up their water tanks and empty their toilets. A small shop called a chandlery sold all the accessories that boaters might want. Zed and Dwain went through the small metal gate onto a gravel path which wound its way round the marina basin. Harry was standing next to a narrowboat on the service point, wearing green overalls and an old black bobble hat.

'Hi 'arry!' Zed waved. Harry looked up from filling the boat with diesel.

'Well there's a surprise, I say, there's a surprise.'

'He always says everything twice.' whispered Zed.

Dwain had never seen so many boats in one place, all different shapes, colours and sizes.

24

'Some people live on 'em all the time.' said Zed. 'Others just moor 'ere for the winter.' He pointed to the small fleet of blue and red boats at the far side of the marina. 'They're the hire boats.' he said. 'That's where Kingfisher is, the one I stowed away on.'

'Well, well,' said Harry. "It's good to see you again young Zed, and who's this. I say, who's this?'

'This is my mate Dwain; we go to school together in London.' said Zed.

'Nice to meet you Dwain, I say nice to meet you. Come on inside and you can tell me what you've been up to in the big city." Zed told Harry about London, and Harry told Zed and Dwain about the news on the canal.

'Before we go 'Arry, is there any chance I could show Dwain 'Kingfisher?'

'Of course, you can, of course you can.' He went into a drawer and pulled out a set of keys, attached to a round cork float.

'There we are, it's the third one along from the end. Be careful of those jetties, they're a bit slippery this time of year.'

Kingfisher was sixty feet long and was moored in between two other hire boats, Swallow and Heron, which were the same length. Kingfisher had a cruiser stern, which meant that there was a large and spacious back deck with the engine underneath the deck's floor boards.

'Come on then.' said Zed, excited to be back on-board Kingfisher.
He unlocked the door and they both walked down the steps into the back cabin.

'Come fru 'ere.' They passed the heads or toilet and went into the kitchen, or galley. Zed pointed to the cabin door at the front, or bow, of the boat.

'This feels really weird. That's where I hid, In the

wardrobe.' he explained to Dwain.

'Ow come nobody saw yer?' asked Dwain.

Zed laughed. 'I waited behind a tree, then, when Peggy got off the boat and went into Jean's shop I jumped on board.'

'Weren't yer scared about what would 'appen if yer got caught?' asked Dwain.

'A bit, but it was better than staying at the circus with me uncle.'

Zed pushed open the front cabin door and Dwain jumped on the double bed.

'This is cool' man, it'd be great to spend a week on 'ere.'

'It's good.' said Zed, 'but I prefer Tim's camper boats.'

'Wait till you see them. 'They are much longer and they 'ave canvas roofs.'

Zed opened the wardrobe door and stood looking inside for a few moments.

'Ow did Peggy know you were in 'ere?' asked Dwain.

'Think I knocked the metal coat 'angers on the rail and they made a noise.'

The boys locked the boat and went back to Harry's office. He was sitting in front of his computer. 'Stupid, stupid, thing, damn modern technology,' he shouted getting ever angrier and red in the face.

'What's up, 'Arry?' asked Zed.

'I'm trying to type this invoice and suddenly it's disappeared off the screen.'

Zed looked over his shoulder. 'Press that, 'Arry.' He did and his work reappeared.

'Well, look at that, magic I say, magic. What a clever lad you are Zed'.

'We do it at school'. he said proudly.

Walking back to the cottage they passed the edge of Coote's Wood.

'They've got two big lakes in there.' said Zed. 'Tim said 'e'd take me fishing there one day.'
Dwain asked why it's called Coote's Wood?
Zed explained that It was owned by this rich bloke, called Mr Coote.'Tim said, 'e never went out and lived in an old broken-down cottage.'

'If I 'ad all that dosh I'd be out spending it.' said Dwain.

'Me too," laughed Zed.

'Where we going now?' asked Dwain.

'I wanna see Jean at the canal shop, it's just up the path from the cottage.
That's where I stowed away on Kingfisher.'

'Cool.' said Dwain, 'though I don't think I would 'ave 'ad the guts.'

Jean was standing on top of a wooden stepladder dusting the shelves. The red brick building that housed the shop was over two hundred years old and had once been a toll house, where load carrying boats would have to pay to go through the lock. Now it sold souvenirs of the waterways; postcards, books, and Peggy's canal art. There was a small section for sweets, groceries and drinks and a whole wall covered in maps and pictures of the waterways. A wooden box held an assortment of short and long handled windlasses for operating the locks, another was full of mooring spikes and long canes with fishing nets at the end. Outside in a large plastic bin were footballs, cricket sets, Frisbees and swing balls. In the back garden, she kept some Rhode Island Red hens and sold the freshly laid eggs in the shop, along with her well known homemade fruit jams and cakes.

On the opposite side of the canal were the old

stables, where the horses, that used to pull the boats along, in the days before they had engines, used to rest overnight. Now it was used by the men who maintained the canal and the lock gates.

She came down the steps and gave Zed a big hug.

'And you must be Dwain.' He smiled. 'Allo, Jean.'

'Right, come on boys. I've got a nice shepherd's pie in the oven."

Dwain whispered to Zed, 'What's a shepherd's pie?'

Zed laughed. 'It's a pie made of shepherds.'

'Don't fancy that, said Dwain pulling a face.

Zed asked Jean if she had been busy in the shop.

'It's starting to pick up now, always does at Easter. There'll be quite a few of

Harry's hire boats coming through soon.' she replied.

Over lunch Jean wanted to hear all about London and school.

Zed asked her if they could go around the back to see Jack the goose.

'Of course, you can.' said Jean. I'd better come with you though, it's been some time since he saw you, and he might chase after you. They don't remember people like dogs do.' She took a bag of popcorn from a shelf. 'He likes this.'

Jack was enclosed in a large wooden pen in the corner of the back garden. The flat roof was made of thick wire mesh, just in case a fox tried his luck in the night. Jean went across to the pen and opened a small wooden gate.

'Now, when he comes out, just stand still, he'll do a lot of hissing and flapping of wings then he'll calm down.' she said.

Nothing happened for a moment then Jack flew out of the pen and across to where the boys were standing. His neck was outstretched and he was hissing loudly.

28

'Oh, shut up Jack.' shouted Jean above the noise. 'It's Zed, he came to see you in the summer, and he's got his friend Dwain with him.'

'Here you are Jack.' said Zed, throwing some popcorn on the floor, Jack stopped hissing and started to eat the popcorn.

'There's a good goose.' said Zed, as he walked over to touch Jack's head.

'Come on Dwain.' he said,'e's alright.' Dwain wasn't convinced and stayed where he was.

After Jack, had eaten all the popcorn Jean shooed him back into his pen.

'Go on, in you go," she said, firmly securing the wooden gate. 'You can't be too careful with these foxes about, cunning little devils.'

'How's Wills?' asked Zed. 'Oh, he's about somewhere.'

Dwain asked who Wills was.

'Jean's black tomcat.' said Zed,'e's huge. Best rat catcher for miles around, leaves 'em on the mat by the back door. They're not always dead though.'

'Rats!' Dwain looked horrified. 'I 'ate rats, I've seen 'em running around by the rubbish bins at our flats.'

Zed laughed. 'There's some big 'uns round 'ere.'

'Oh, don't tell him stories, Zed.' scolded Jean, 'you'll frighten the poor boy.'

She assured Dwain that it was only field mice Wills hunted.'

' Did you know Mr Coote who owned the woods Jean?' asked Zed.

She nodded. 'I did. Kept himself to himself though, he didn't have any visitors, was a bit of a recluse.'

Dwain asked her what a recluse was.

She told him that it was a person who lives alone, and avoids other people.

29

'But wasn't he lonely?" asked Zed.

'I expect he was.' replied Jean. 'As far as I know, the only person he ever saw was Rose. She used to get his shopping and do his washing. She did that for years, right up until he died last year.'

'Where does Rose live?' asked Zed.

'On a narrowboat, moored near Muckle Farm. Peggy knows her very well.'

She took some freshly made cakes from the counter and put them in a bag.

'Now I think it's time you were heading back before it gets dark. Give these to Peggy for me, and don't eat them on the way home.'

Zed laughed. 'We won't, promise.'

'It's been nice to meet you Dwain.' said Jean, opening the shop door.

'And you.' said Dwain, 'and thanks for the sheep pie.'

'Shepherds.' called Zed, laughing as he kicked an old football down the garden.

Jean chuckled and went inside.

It was only a short distance from the shop to the cottage and although it was nearly dark the boys were in no hurry to get back. Sitting on a low brick wall they watched as a silvery mist settled on the canal. Two grey squirrels were chasing each other along a thin branch which hung dangerously low over the water.

'Do you think they can swim?' asked Dwain scanning the towpath for a missile.

'Ope not'. replied Zed, 'Tim reckons they're vermin, that's why there's no red ones left.'

'Didn't know they 'ad red ones.' said Dwain, throwing a large stone towards the branch and hoping to knock one off.

'Let's see if they can swim.' he laughed.

30

'Hello boys.'

They were so engrossed in watching the squirrels they hadn't seen the rough looking man coming around the bend.

'You two local to 'ere?'

Zed stood up. 'Sort of.' he replied.

'What's that mean, sort of?' asked the man.

'We only come down here in the holidays.'

The man walked closer to the boys. 'Right, well do yer know a place called Coote's Wood?'

'Yeah, it's along the towpath.' Zed said, pointing in that general direction.

'I'm looking for a woman who used to visit old Mr Coote regular like."

'Who's that then?' asked Zed, looking at Dwain.

The man shook his head. 'Don't know 'er name, thought you might.'

Now a local boy, knowing the answer, might well have offered it up, but Zed was from London, and there, particularly where he lived, nobody readily admitted to knowing anything. If it smelt funny, it was probably bad.

'Why do you want to know?' Zed asked cheekily.

'Never mind that. Do you know 'er or not?' he replied raising his voice.

Zed thought for a moment. 'No idea, mate. Sorry.'

'You sure about that son?' he said. Zed noticed he had tattoos across the fingers of his nicotine stained hands just like his uncle Darren.

'Yeah, I am.' said Zed, pushing past him. 'We gotta go, come on Dwain.'

Suddenly the man grabbed Zed's arm, 'Don't forget the bag Zed.'

Zed froze, how did he know his name, who was he? He grabbed the bag of cakes from the wall and they both ran back to the cottage.

When they burst through the kitchen door, Peggy was not in a happy mood.

'Where have you been? It's nearly dark, and well past six.'

They had run so fast they were finding it hard to breathe.

'It was this man Peg.' spluttered Zed, hardly able to speak.

'On the towpath. E wanted to know if we knew Coote's Wood, and if we knew Rose, you know, who used to work for old Mr Coote and, and...........'

'Calm down boy.' said Peggy firmly. 'Sit down and take a breath.'

Zed sat on the sofa next to Dwain.

'E new my name Peg, and I ain't never seen 'im before.'Ow did 'e know my name?'

'You're sure he's not from the village?' asked Peg.

'I'm sure.' said Zed, 'and 'e 'ad tattoos on 'is fingers just like me uncle.'

Peggy pulled up a chair next to the sofa.

'That doesn't mean anything Zed. Lots of people have tattoos, and they are not all like your uncle, although this is very odd, I'll grant you that.'

'And 'e didn't talk like you.' said Dwain suddenly.

'What do you mean love?' asked Peggy.

'You know.' said Dwain, 'you all sort of talk funny down 'ere. 'E talked like they do where we live."

'Do you mean with a London accent?' asked Peggy.

'Yeah, s'pose so.' said Dwain looking at Zed.

Peggy thought for a moment.

'Let's wait until Tim gets home and see what he thinks. In the meantime, I have just the thing to take your mind off it'. Opening a draw in the kitchen she produced two potato peelers.

'Oh, and, Jean sent these for you.' said Zed

32

producing a crumpled bag of cakes.

Peggy laughed. 'What did you do, sit on them?'

'Sorry, it was when we were running, I dropped them.' said Zed.

'And I trod on 'em.' said Dwain sheepishly.

Peggy plonked a large bag of potatoes on the table.

'Well I expect we can salvage something from them, although they are a bit squashed. I'm going to get some logs. We need to build the fire up before Tim comes home.' Peggy went outside and returned carrying two armfuls of logs from the garden. She placed them in front of the fireplace. 'Brrr, it's cold out there.' she said turning towards where the boys were sitting.

'STOP, STOP.' she shouted. 'What are you doing to those potatoes?'

Startled the boys looked up.

'Peeling 'em.' replied Zed, 'like you asked us to.'

'You're only supposed to cut the peel off, not demolish half of the potato.'

She grabbed the peelers from their hands, then took a deep breath.

'Right change of plan boys, you go outside and get more logs, I'll do the potatoes.'

The boys didn't need telling twice and quickly ran outside.

It was about an hour later when they heard Tim's Land Rover coming up the bumpy track. He had been at Boswell's Yard all day. Barney was first through the door and made straight for his bowl.

'Shall I give Barney his dinner Peg?' asked Zed.

'Please love. He can also have some of the stew after we've eaten.'

'How did it go?' Peggy asked.

Tim pulled off his boots and dirty overalls. 'Fine.' he said. 'We had a good clear up then opened the paddles, so the dock will be filled by tomorrow.'

'Well dinner's nearly ready. Do you want to have a shower first?'

'Yes, I really need one.' he said, making for the bedroom.

Peggy called after him. 'You'd better take this.' She threw him a large bath towel.

Zed and Dwain sat on the sofa in front of the roaring fire, while Peggy checked on the stew.

They both found it strange having to sit at a table to eat. Back home they always had their meals on trays watching the television. Peggy, however, insisted that they sat at the table which was laid with place mats and cloth napkins.

'So, what you been up to today?' asked Tim.

Peggy butted in. 'They've got something to tell you about.'

'Oh yes. What's that then?' said Tim, putting a spoonful of lamb stew into his mouth. Zed explained how Jean at the shop had told them about old Mr Coote, and how someone called Rose who was moored near Muckle Farm was the only person who ever visited him.

'That's right.' said Tim, 'she went to see him every day, never missed.'

Then Zed told Tim about the rough looking man they had met on the towpath, and how he was asking if they knew Rose.

'But 'e didn't know 'er name.' interrupted Dwain.

'No, 'e just said do we know the woman who used to visit old Mr Coote.

And 'e knew my name,' said Zed getting louder.''Ow did he know my name Tim, when I ain't ever seen him before?'

Peggy interrupted. 'It's haven't love, not ain't, and how starts with an H.'

34

'Well quite a few people in the village know you stay here now, maybe one of them has mentioned your name.' said Tim, not seeming particularly concerned.

'You must admit it seems a bit odd.' said Peggy, 'particularly as the boys say he spoke with a London accent. And why would anyone be asking about Rose?'
Tim wiped up the last of his stew with a piece of bread. 'Might be a long lost relative.' he said.

'Well if that was the case, he'd know her name, wouldn't he?' replied Peggy sharply.

'I'll have an ask round tomorrow, see if anyone else has seen him about, I wouldn't worry about it boys, probably never see him again.'

'Op not'. said Zed, he was creepy.'

There was no moon that night and the cold dark air pressed heavily against the window. Somewhere in the distance an owl called to the night. Dwain had dropped off quickly, but Zed had trouble sleeping. He listened as water seeped through the gap between the lock gates, before tumbling onto the concrete cill below. How very different from his gran's flat in London, where even in the early hours of the morning you could hear the noise of the traffic from the road below, but it never kept him awake as he was used to it.

Here the silence seemed deafening, and he was still wondering who the man on the towpath was. He waved his hand in front of his face, nothing, only blackness. He moved it closer until it touched his nose, but still he couldn't see it. It must be like this if you are blind, he thought, or dead. 'Ow horrible.'

'One, two, three, four, five.' he started to count sheep but got bored after fifty. His gran had told him to do this if he couldn't sleep, although he never understood why it had to be sheep jumping over a fence. Why not pigs? They must be able to jump a bit, or horses? They can

35

certainly jump. He decided to count kangaroos, as they can hop higher

'One kangaroo, two kangaroo, three kangaroo, four kangaroo zzzzzzzzz'

Rocket Ron woke at eight o clock. The rain was beating on the roof of his narrow boat, Neptune. Walking through to the galley, he undid the catch on the door of the small wooden cage where he kept Frankie and Freddie his two ferrets.

Ron made himself a cup of tea.'

'Come on, get up you two'. he shouted kicking the side of their cage. Outside it was wet and dull. He hated this weather as it played havoc with his arthritic legs. Picking up his old waterproof coat and hat he let Frankie and Freddie out onto the muddy towpath.

'Walkies!' he called and the two ferrets scampered along the towpath in front of him, often disappearing into the deep puddles. Muckle Farm near Bridge 27 was only a short distance away. Ron always kept an eye on the old place. He had many happy memories of when it was a working dairy farm. His friends Pauline and Ralph Collins had owned the farm, as had Ralph's parents before them. Then foot and mouth disease arrived and wiped out their herd of dairy cows, and with it their livelihood. Now all that remained was the empty farmhouse and the feed storage barn. The gate which led into the farm yard swung to and fro, clinging to the post by one corroded hinge. He passed the mooring where Rose kept her boat, Spirit. He would call on her on the way back to pick up his potion. Frankie and Freddie had scampered ahead and were playing underneath an old rusty tractor. The rain was getting heavier so Rocket Ron decided to take shelter under the wooden porch over the front door. It was a large porch where waterproofs and boots would have been kept.

'That's odd, he said to Frankie and Freddie. The padlock and hasp had been broken off. He gently pushed open the creaking door and walked slowly into the deserted kitchen. Frankie and Freddie had climbed onto the old kitchen table and were chasing each other around in circles, throwing clouds of dust up behind them. Ron noticed that in the corner of the room was the remains of a fire. He touched the burnt logs to see if there was any warmth, but they were cold. Must be tramps or kids, he thought.

'Come on, you two,' he called to Frankie and Freddie, 'let's go and see Rose. It's colder in here than outside.'

Rose had got up early. She knew that Rocket Ron was coming to collect his herbal potions, for his aching legs. Opening the door to let her two cats, Woody and Foggy, out, she saw a little brown bear sitting on the grass in front of the boat.

He was soaking wet, with one of his little arms hanging on by the thinnest of threads.

'My, my.' said Rose, bending down to pick him up.

'You do look in a right old state!' She carried him into the boat and placed him on a stool. 'Now you sit there while I find something to clean you up with.'

Rose was a Paganus, meaning country dweller or rustic. She was very spiritual and believed with a passion in the power of natural therapies to cure all ills. Others were less kind and thought she was a bit batty. She would often take the secret path through the woods to gather plants and herbs to make her potions.

On entering her boat there was a strong smell of cooking herbs and scented candles. The roof inside was painted black like the night sky, illuminated by a twinkling moon and stars. Shelves were piled with books on Druids,

Wiccans, and Shamans. On the wooden table stood a set of old-fashioned scales to weigh the herbs, and a pestle and mortar for crushing the herbs into powder before making them into a potion.

Rocket Ron tapped on the galley window. 'You in there Rose?'

She quickly opened the door. 'Come in my dear you must be freezing.'

Frankie and Freddie made straight for the warmth of the stove. Ron made himself   comfortable in a wooden rocking chair.

'Where did he come from?' asked Ron, as Rose dried the little bear in an old towel.

'No idea, he was just sitting there on the grass when I let the cats out.

That's how most of the bears have arrived over the years. I'll clean him up and mend his arm then he can go in the trunk with the others until the spring.'

'And how are the others?' asked Rocket.

'Very good, still in hibernation though. They're in there if you want to see them.' She pointed to the large wooden trunk under the table.

Ron lifted the lid. Inside were dozens of teddies, of all ages and sizes.

'Just think.' said Rose, 'every one of them has a story to tell. Who did they belong to? Where did they come from? What age are they? Wouldn't it be fascinating to know?'

'When was the first one left?' asked Ron.

'Oh, about twenty years ago. That was Dibble, he's an old man now, and sits at the top of the bear tree.'

Outside her boat stood five magnificent weeping willows trees. Further along was another willow, but much smaller, its blackened branches pointing in all directions, like a sign post. This was the bear tree. Rose would tell visitors how the willow is the tree of dreaming and deep emotions; that it symbolises growth and vitality. Before the night of the great storm, when the tree was struck by lightning, she had made her willow wand from one of its branches. When spring, the season of re-birth approaches she places all the little bears on the tree and touches them with the willow wand. Once loved, now abandoned, it is said that when people sleep, the bears come alive and play together at the base of the willow tree.

Rocket Ron had heard this story many times, and unlike some, who put it down to her battiness he liked to imagine it to be true, and that all those little bears have found happiness at last.

Rose closed the trunk. 'Fancy a cuppa?

'Could murder one thanks'

'And how have the legs been?' called Rose from the galley.

'A lot better since I been taking that potion you gave me. I even helped Tim take the boats to Boswell's in the week, and was crossing over the locks like a young un.'

'Well I've made you up another bottle," said Rose, putting two steaming mugs of tea on the table.

Ron asked her if she had seen anyone hanging about recently?

'Like who?'

'I don't know, replied Ron, but I was up at Muckle Farm before I came here, and someone had knocked the lock off the kitchen door, and there were the remains of a fire in the kitchen.'

'Local kids or tramps.' said Rose.

'That's what I thought.' replied Ron. 'Best keep an eye out though, there's some odd people about these days.'

After Ron and the ferrets had left Rose picked up the little bear and sewed his torn arm back to his body.

'There, little fella, a nice new arm.' She put the little bear on the stool by the fire. 'All we need to do now is dry you out, then you can make friends with the other bears in the trunk.'

CHAPTER FOUR

Are there ghosts?

Are there ghosts on the waterways?   Of course, why would you think otherwise?
Those ghostly apparitions that slip silently between the two worlds. Sit quietly at the edge of the canal, just as dusk turns to darkness. Close your eyes so you are at one

with them. Soon you will hear the slow thud of the horse's hooves on the towpath, its nostrils steaming as it exhales heavily, slowly pulling the loaded boat along towards the lock. You will hear the strain on the rope, the sudden snap of tension as any slack is taken up, the shout as the boatman calls to Albert to make the lock ready.

He'll be looking for you, Albert Wilks wearing a black waistcoat and carrying an oil lantern, with his windlass pushed inside his sturdy leather belt, which holds up his worn trousers. He is puffing a clay pipe; he's always puffing a clay pipe! using the tobacco the boatmen bring him from London.

You are a stranger to his canal, to his lock, and his cottage. But he'll be smiling, glad you are here and taking an interest in the waterways. For over a hundred and fifty years now he has revisited this place, where he lived and manned this lock. He knew all the boatmen and their families who passed through, as they travelled to London, where they would unload their wares onto ships in Lime House dock, then re- load and return.

They mean you no harm. Having journeyed into the long dark tunnel that all boatmen will eventually pass through, occasionally they return to the places they were familiar with.

But beware of the ghost of Black Jack. He is a different type of spirit. In life he was a blaggard, a pirate, who, with his wife, One Legged Laura, used to hold up and rob the boatmen as they came through the top lock at Melbury There was a tall pine tree, at least a hundred feet high. Black Jack would climb up into the branches so he could see the boats coming, then, when they were in the lock and the gates were shut, he would jump from the tree onto the lock gate, and with two drawn pistols demand their money or their lives. One Legged Laura would hold the horses and keep watch. None of the boaters were armed so they had no choice but to hand everything over. The robbers would then gallop away to their hideout until the next time.

Word of the robberies spread quickly along the canal and soon the boatmen were fearful of travelling along this stretch, in case they were held up at Melbury by Black Jack and One-Legged Laura. Wealthy merchant Sir Henry Portas, had become concerned that this pirate, Black Jack, was affecting the movement of cargo to and from London, and of course his profits. He decided to call a meeting in the Blue Anchor tavern, of all the merchants whose goods were moved by canal to London.

A merchant ship called the Athlone Star had docked in the harbour that same day and was being unloaded of its cargo of cotton and tobacco. The crew, of rough, tough men, had been at sea for months, and were in the Blue Anchor tavern getting drunk, and eyeing the ladies. That night, in the tavern on the harbour side, Sir Henry Portas seized his chance, and Black Jack's fate was sealed. The following day four of the seamen, more used to the pitch and roll of a ship, than a galloping horse, rode out towards the lock at Melbury.In the pay of Sir Henry Portas and the other rich merchants, their mission was to eliminate Black Jack and one-Legged Laura.

They made camp in the woods alongside the top lock at Melbury, where they would wait until Black Jack and One Legged Laura'appeared. Days passed, and they were beginning to wonder if Black Jack would return. Then one evening, just as the sun was falling behind the vales and the light starting to fade, a lone boat slid quietly from the bend in the canal and moored at the bottom lock. The boatman walked slowly up to the lock, placing his windlass on the spindle before turning it to lift the paddles. Water rushed and swirled around the hull of the boat as the lock emptied out its contents into the canal.

The boatman's wife kept a firm hold on the towing horse.

A shout came from high up in the pine tree, where one of the men had been keeping a lookout for Black Jack and one-legged Laura. Coming fast, they both galloped across the muddy fields towards the lock and its waiting prize. Creeping closer, the men cocked their pistols and waited while the horse pulled the boat into the lock. Suddenly a figure dressed from head to toe in black, and wearing a mask to hide his face, appeared from the cover of the trees on the opposite side of the lock.

'Hand over yer money now.' he shouted, waving a pair of pistols at the terrified boatman and his wife. But before the boatmen could take his purse from his pocket, two men burst from the woods, at other side of the lock, and ran towards Black Jack. Distracted, he turned towards them, not seeing the third man who had crept up behind him. He aimed his pistol and shot Black Jack through the back of the head. Hearing the shots One Legged Laura tried to escape on one of the horses, but as she mounted, the fourth man pulled her from the horse and shot her through the heart. Sir Henry Portas had said that they should be made an example of, so ropes were tied to their feet and they were both hauled upside down into the tree, where their bodies were left to rot, as a warning to any other robbers.

Now, on that day every year, just as the sun dips below the dales and the light fades Black Jack returns to that place. His troubled spirit full of rage at those who killed him and his own stupidity in getting caught. Sometimes he is seen high in the pine tree or standing on the lock gate, with pistols drawn. Nobody's ever seen One Legged Laura though. Maybe in spirit she has deserted the man who she loved, but who led her to a gruesome death.

44

Peggy had taken the boys to see Rose. She wanted to ask her about the man on the towpath. It was also troubling that he knew Zed's name. Tim was going fishing, so he had dropped them off at the end of the lane that led to the swing bridge. Running ahead of Peggy, the boys, took a short cut through a small copse and across the garden of the Waterside Café, which was closed for the winter.

'Is that the swing bridge?' asked Dwain.

'Yeah, it's the only one on this stretch of the canal.' replied Zed.

'Ow does it work?'

Zed explained that it used to be opened by a large wheel, which the boaters had to turn by hand, but now it's operated by electricity.

'See that metal box on that wooden post, well, you open it with a special key, then push the buttons inside and it swings open.'

'Bet the car drivers get really fed up 'aving to wait till the boats go through.' said Dwain laughing.

'They do.' replied Zed, 'particularly in the summer when there are lots of boats using the canal.'

Standing on the swing bridge they waited until Peggy caught them up.

'Blimey you've got some energy.' she puffed.'

They walked the short distance along the towpath, passing Muckle Farm, before arriving at Rose's boat, Spirit, moored by the five willow trees.

Sitting round the wooden table Zed and Dwain listened intently, as Rose told them stories of the ghosts who haunt the canal. Every so often she would stop talking and run her long bony fingers through her white hair, which hung down to her waist.

Zed said he wouldn't mind seeing the friendly ghosts, but not Black Jack.

'I still don't see 'ow people who've died can come

45

back from the dead.' Said Dwain.

Rose smiled. 'Well they're dead in a physical form dear, but not in a spiritual way.'

'But where do they go?' asked Zed.

'They don't really go anywhere.' replied Rose, 'they just pass over into another dimension, on a different vibration.'

Zed got up and stood behind Peggy making ghostly noises. 'I could come back and haunt you Peg.' he shouted.

'No chance," laughed Peggy, 'they wouldn't let you back again. Once is enough for anybody.'

Zed asked if they could have a look round outside.

'Go on then.' said Peggy, 'and don't get up to any mischief.'

Rose called after them. 'Don't be too long, lunch is nearly ready.'

'Race yer to the bend.' said Dwain, laughing and running off.

'That's not fair.' shouted Zed following him, 'you've already started.'

Sitting on a fallen tree they waved as a boat went slowly by.

'People are really nice on the canal.' said Dwain, 'not like London where they ignore yer all the time.'

'Yeah, they always wave and say 'allo.' replied Zed.

'Those must be the willows she was telling us about.' said Zed as they walked back to the boat.

'Do yer think she's sort of, like a witch?' asked Dwain.

Zed shrugged. 'She's a bit weird, that stuff about bears coming alive at night. I 'ad a bear once and it never came alive.'

Dwain asked what he meant.

46

Zed laughed, as he swung on a low willow branch.''Cos I threw it out of the window of the flat. Splat.'

The boys ran back to the boat laughing.

'Ah, just in time.' said Rose, holding a plate with four large cheese and potato pasties on it.

'Did you make those?' asked Zed.

'I did indeed, just for you, though I had to be careful in case one of the bears got there first. They love my pasties.'

The boys grinned at each other. 'Told you she's a witch.' whispered Dwain.

Peggy waited until they were all sitting down with their lunch.

'Rose, there's something I need to ask you.'

Twisting the rings on her long bony fingers, Rose thought for a long time before responding to Peggy's question.

'I couldn't say love, can't think why anyone would want to talk to me about Mr Coote. All I did was get his shopping and do his washing. And you say he didn't ask for me by name.'

Zed shook his head. 'No 'e didn't but 'e knew mine.'

'That is odd, I grant you. Maybe he heard it from someone in the village, you know how people gossip round here.'

'Then why would he be asking about you Rose?' asked Peggy,

'We're only assuming it's me dear.'

'Course it's you Rose, nobody else ever visited him.'

Rose shrugged her shoulders. 'Then I'm at a loss dear, sorry.'

'You are sure?' asked Peggy.

'Quite sure, my dear. Now let's make a nice cup of tea, and I'm sure you two would like some homemade lemonade.'

47

Tim had arranged to pick them up on the main road, on his way back from fishing at the lakes.

They crossed the swing bridge and walked back up the narrow lane towards the lay-by on main road.

'Betsy's coming.' laughed Zed.

Peggy shook her head. 'It sounds like an old tank.' she said irritably, 'I wish he'd get that exhaust pipe fixed before it falls off.'

'You all right Peg?' asked Zed, touching her arm.

'I'm ok love, just worried about Rose.'

Betsy shuddered to a halt in the small lay-by. As Peggy opened the passenger door, Barney leapt off the front seat, and ran to join the boys in the back.

'Ah! Get off, you're all wet.' shouted Zed, as Barney jumped on them both.

'He's been swimming in the lake.' laughed Tim.

'Have we got fish for dinner tonight then?' asked Peggy.

Tim laughed. 'The only thing I caught was a cold.'

'Hear that boys.' she called, 'we've got nothing to eat tonight.'

'Oh great.' said Zed, 'I'm starving.'

'Just as well I put a stew in the slow burner before we left.' said Peggy.

Closing her eyes, she rested her head on the back of the seat when suddenly two loud bangs came from underneath the Land Rover.

'Good grief, what on earth was that?' she shouted, jumping out of the seat.

'Sounds like guns going off.' called Dwain.

Zed was holding Barney, who was frightened and trying to jump out of the back.

'Calm down, calm down.' yelled Tim. It's only the exhaust pipe blowing.'

'Only!' shouted Peggy, 'I nearly had a heart attack.

48

Then what would you do?'

Tim laughed. 'Don't worry, I'll give you the kiss of life.'

Peggy shook her head and sighed in exasperation. 'Just get the thing fixed before
you get nicked.'

CHAPTER FIVE

Bringing the boats back

Boswells Yard to Shimington Tunnel

Nothing much had changed at Boswell's Yard since Zed was last there. The old rusting lorry with the crane on the back was still there. Jack Boswell used this to lift boats in and out of the water. At one end of the yard was a pile of old engines that had been taken out of boats, and a big mobile generator for producing electricity. There were stacks of sheet steel for repairing boats and Zed noticed that Rex, the German Shepherd dog, that lived in the kennel had gone. Zed didn't have happy memories of this place. This is where they had finished the journey on 'Kingfisher' two years ago, and from where Zed was to be sent back home to London, possibly never seeing Peggy, Tim and Barney again.

'You start unpacking.' said Tim. 'I'll go and see Jack Boswell; I need to pay him some money.' Tim and Barney walked to the large caravan that Jack used as an office and home. Jack was wrestling with the door of a filing cabinet which had jammed. Nothing had improved in here either. The desk was still covered with bundles of paper, and the floor was littered with used plastic cups.

'I don't know how you can work in this mess.' said Tim.

Jack laughed. 'It may look like a mess to you, but I know where everything is.'

'Right.' said Tim, smiling. Barney was enjoying some discarded cat meat that he had found in a dish.

Jack had now resorted to beating the drawer with a hammer to open it.

'Tell you what.' said Tim, 'why don't you let me open that, while you sort out my Invoice?'

'Good plan mate," said Jack, laying the hammer on the floor. 'Now where did I put that invoice?'

Tim shook his head and smiled.

Carrying his ruck-sack and sleeping bag, Zed opened the door that led into the dry dock. Odin and Thor were sitting in the flooded dock, their recently painted black hulls shining under the florescent roof lights. Undoing the guy straps on Odin, Zed threw his bag inside, then climbed down the wooden steps into the galley area. Dwain followed.

'Wow man, this is really cool.' said Dwain. They're really big.'

'They look a lot bigger in 'ere.' said Zed.

'You two, go and get the rest of the stuff from the Land Rover." called Peggy handing Zed two bags of food for the journey. 'And don't forget Tim's tool box, or we'll never hear the last of it.'

Peggy climbed inside and started putting the shopping into the cupboards

'How that man keeps this place running I'll never know. He can't find a dam thing.' grumbled Tim, as he followed Barney down the steps.

'Can you light the stove?' asked Peggy. 'It's a bit chilly in here.'

Tim went out into the dock and returned with a large bag of coal.

'I've put three more bags on Thor. That should last us, and we can pick some logs up on the way.'

'These are really 'eavy.' shouted Zed, dropping Tim's tools onto the side of the dock.

'It's heavy with an H.' called Peggy from down below.

Tim lifted the tools into the boat and the boys jumped inside.

'Right then.' said Tim, 'first things first, engine checks. Come on you two.'

The boys followed Tim to the stern end of Thor.

'Ok Zed, what's our method for checking?' asked Tim.

'It's F.O.W.E B.A.G.S.' said Zed proudly.

Tim nodded. 'Very good, now can you remember what they stand for.'

Zed thought for a moment.

'Fuel, Oil, Water.' He hesitated. 'Ang on, 'ang on,' he said, thinking.

'Electrics.'

Good lad, said Tim, 'carry on.'

'Bilges, Anchor, G-G-G what is G? Grease gland" he shouted, pumping his fist into the air.

'One more to go'. said Tim smiling.

'Easy peesy," said Zed, 'Steering.'

Tim laughed. 'Well done that man, ding. Thank you for playing. Now you can show Dwain where they all are, while I go and light the stove before Peggy starts nagging me.'

''Ow did you remember all those? asked Dwain.

'Just learnt 'em since I first came 'ere. Tim's really strict about checking everything before you move the boat.'

When the boys went down below Tim had lit the stove, and the inside of the boat was warm and cosy. Peggy had made some sandwiches and soup for lunch, and Barney was chewing on a large bone that Tim had got for him. He growled when Zed got too near. "I don't want the smelly thing," said Zed, poking him with his foot.

'Ok', let's do it,' said Tim finishing his sandwich. 'Time and tide………..'

'Wait for no one.' shouted Zed.

'Quite right. Now you get your buoyancy aids on while I get her started."

Zed could never understand why Tim used that saying, as there was no tide on the canal. Peggy walked to open the gates at the front of the dock.

Zed showed Dwain how to put the buoyancy aid on, then they went to the stern of Odin where Tim was putting the shiny brass handled tiller bar on.

'That's what you steer with.' he said to Dwain.

Thor's tiller bar was made of thick wood, and curved

53

upwards at the end. It was longer than Odin's and was painted in bright colours. Tim walked to the bow of Odin and undid the line that attached the boat to the dock.

'Ok Zed, untie the stern line.' he called, walking back, 'and show Dwain how to coil it up.' Peggy had done the same with the stern lines on Thor.

Tim stepped on board and pushed the throttle forward. Slowly Odin moved towards the end of the dock. When the stern of Odin was level with the bow of Thor, he tied the stern line of Odin onto the front of Thor.

'Ready?' he shouted to Peggy who was standing with Dwain on the stern of the butty Thor.

'Ready," she called. There was a sudden jolt as Odin lurched forward, taking up the slack in the towline. Tim and Peggy pushed hard over on the tiller bars so as not to hit the bank opposite as the boats came around. Zed had to duck quickly under the tiller bar, to avoid being knocked overboard.

'Great.' shouted Tim, 'we're on our way.'

'That was brill Peg.' said Dwain. 'I didn't think you'd make that turn.'

Peggy smiled. 'We've been doing it for some time now love.'

Tim pushed the throttle forward to increase the speed of Odin's powerful engine. A dull sky hung over the surrounding fallow fields, winter trees, their branches shorn since last autumns fall, shivered and shook in the chilly breeze. Small birds rapidly darted to and fro before seeking shelter in the high hedgerows which lined the sides of the canal. Gulls screamed, and swooped across recently ploughed furrows in search of fat worms.

The boys were glad of their new blue woollen hats that Peggy had bought them, with 'First Mate' written on the front in red. Tim had said she should have got the ones with 'Galley Slaves' on. Dwain liked the tall steel pylons, with their outstretched arms gripping the buzzing cables, that carried electricity beyond the horizon. He said they were like aliens all marching in a line to destroy London. Peggy asked him why London.

'I 'ate the place, it's a dump, much better 'ere.' She smiled.

They passed under Three Arches Bridge and around the sweeping bend, where a group of fishermen, evenly paced along the bank, reluctantly raised their long fishing poles, which reached to the opposite bank. Tim waved and called 'thanks,' as they passed, but got no response.

'Pig ignorant.' he said to Zed.

'Are they always that miserable?' asked Dwain.

'Mostly.' replied Peggy laughing. 'Mind you if I were sitting freezing on a cold canal bank and not catching anything, I would probably be grumpy'.

'Especially if yer weren't catching anything.' laughed Dwain.

Zed shouted. 'Lock ahead.'

Beecham Wood Lock was one of ten they would pass through on their journey home to Tiddledurn.

'Why do they 'ave 'em? asked Dwain.

'What love?' asked Peggy, keeping Thor in a straight line behind Odin.

'The locks.'

Peggy explained. 'It's how you move the water up and down hills, love.'

Tim eased the throttle back to slow Odin down.

'Take the tiller Zed, and keep it straight.'

'You ready Peg?' he shouted over the noise of Odin's engine.

Peggy waved. 'Ready.'

He waited until Thor drifted to where he was standing at the stern of Odin. Once the towline had slackened he bent down, and undid it from the cleat, coiling it in his hand.

Pushing the bow of Thor to the starboard, or right-hand side of Odin, he then walked along the starboard gunwales holding the line. He didn't need to pull on the line as Thor's momentum enabled it to glide alongside Odin. When both boats were level with each other he tied, Thor's bowline to the cleat on the front of Odin. Dwain held the wooden tiller bar of Thor while Peggy secured the stern end.

Taking the tiller from Zed, Tim tweaked the throttle and steered the boats alongside the mooring just below the lock gates. Zed jumped off and tied Odin's bow line to a mooring ring that was set in the bank. Tim did the same with the stern line. The lock chamber was empty, so all they had to do was open the gates, then Tim could steer the boats in.

'Cor, they only just fit.' said Dwain.
When the bottom gates were closed, they walked to the gates at the other end of the lock.

'You show Dwain what to do here.' said Peggy. 'I'll cross over to the other side.'
Zed placed his windlass on the spindle at the side of the ground paddles.

'Make sure the 'clicker' as he called it, is resting on the ratchet. That stops the windlass spinning round if yer let go of it.' he told Dwain.

'Ready Tim?' shouted Peggy.
Tim waved. 'Ready.'
As Zed and Peggy turned the windlass, the paddles in the lock gates started to lift and the water from the canal flooded into the lock chamber.
Zed passed the windlass to Dwain. ''Ere, 'ave a go.'
Dwain placed the windlass on the spindle.

'Turn it then'. he said laughing.
'I'm trying. It's really 'ard.' he puffed.
Peggy shouted to them. 'More porridge for you two.'

'It's not me.' protested Zed, 'its Dwain, he's got no strength.'

Peggy laughed, 'I seem to remember someone else struggling with them once.'

'Oh, yeah, whatever.' said Zed, taking the windlass off the spindle.

They both leaned their bums on the balance beam while the lock flooded. Zed told Dwain that there was no point in pushing, as the gates won't open until the water level in the lock is the same as the canal.

'You'll feel a little tremor in the beam.' he said, 'then we can push it open.'

Tim steered the boats out and moored them alongside the bank. Peggy and the boys closed the gates and wound down the paddles.

'Well done Dwain.' called Peggy, 'you've done your first lock. Don't forget to take the windlass with you.'

'Why don't you two walk Barney to the next lock, give him some exercise?' called Tim pushing the stern of Odin away from the bank.

''Ow far is it?' shouted Zed.

'Only two miles.' laughed Tim, steering the boats to the middle of the canal.

'Two miles! said Dwain, sounding horrified.

'Ain't never walked two miles in me life.'

'Come on Barney.' said Zed, patting him on the head, 'we've been conned.'

They ran the first 100 meters before Dwain stopped for a pee. Barney had run ahead and was staring through a gate at a flock of scrawny sheep huddling together to keep warm.

'Can't get through there Zed can, e?'

Zed chuckled. 'He wouldn't know what to do if 'e did. Never 'ad to round anything up 'ave yer mate.'

At the end of the long straight they could see the stern ends of Thor and Odin disappearing around the next bend. They crossed over a white wooden bridge where a fast stream emptied out into the canal. It was quite muddy underfoot, and they had to pick their way slowly between the deep puddles and the thick grass at the edge of the canal.

'So, yer like it down ere Dwain?'

'Its great man, makes yer realise what a dump London is though.'

'I hate 'aving to go back there.' said Zed. 'When I finish school, I'm going to come and live 'ere with Tim and Peggy.'

Dwain laughed, 'or get chucked out first.'

'No way. They wouldn't let me come any more if I did that, it was part of the deal we made.'

'What deal?'

'They said I could come in the holidays, only if I worked hard at school.'

'What will yer do if yer move down 'ere?'

Zed picked up a stick and threw it for Barney. 'Work with Tim and Peg on the boats, he'd learn me to be a mechanic if I asked.

'Teach.' said Dwain loudly.

'What?'

Dwain shook his head. 'It's teach, not learn. See, some of us listen in English.'

'Yeah well, it's not my best subject.' laughed Zed, 'and I don't like that Miss   Steel, 'er breath stinks when she leans over yer.'

'Let's run.' said Dwain, as a cold shiver ran through his body.

Then Zed's phone rang.

'It's probably Peggy telling us to hurry up.' he said.

''Allo'

For a moment he said nothing. 'Yeah, I'm ok.'

Zed paused. 'Ow did yer get this number?'

'Yeah, that's right.'

'Why? Dunno, we got a lot on.'

'I'll ask 'em, I gotta go now, see yer.'

Zed looked shaken.

'Who was that?' asked Dwain.

'Me uncle. Can't believe me gran gave him the number. 'E wanted to know if I was staying with Tim and Peggy, and said he'd like to see me.'

''Ow does 'e know about this place then?' asked Dwain.

''E comes 'ere with the circus every year.'

Zed started to run towards the lock where Tim and Peggy would be waiting for them.

''Ang on, shouted Dwain running after him. Barney was close on Zed's heels.

'And 'e wants me to ask if 'e can visit.' Zed shouted over his shoulder.

'What, down 'ere?' puffed Dwain.

Peggy and Tim had already worked the boats through the lock and were sitting at the stern drinking from mugs of tea.

'Come on slow coaches.' she called.

'Just 'ad a phone call.' said Zed. 'It was me uncle.'

Peggy was surprised. 'Where did he get your number?'

'Said Gran gave it to him.'

'Why would she do that? asked Peggy.

Tim was concerned. 'What did he want?'

'You tell Tim about it,' said Peggy, 'while I go and make you both a nice mug of hot chocolate. You look frozen. Come on Barney let's find you a biscuit.'

'I thought it was Peggy ringing to tell us to get a move on. 'E asked if I was alright, and if I was staying

59

down 'ere with you and Peg.'

'What did you say?' asked Tim.

Zed bent down and removed a stone from his trainer. 'Said I was. Then he said he wanted to see me, and could I ask if he can come down.'

'Damn cheek.' said Tim angrily. 'Didn't give a fig about you for two years, now he suddenly wants to see you.'

'E's up to something'. said Zed, 'I know 'im.'

Peggy called the boys down below to have their hot chocolate and biscuits.

'What do yer think 'e wants Peg?' asked Zed.

She shook her head. 'I don't know love, though it's strange that he should surface now. I'll speak to your gran, see if she can throw any light on it. In the meantime, if he rings again don't answer it.'

The canal widened as they left Beecham Wood Lock. Soon they would be passing through several narrow bridge holes so Tim and Peggy dropped Thor behind Odin into the towing position. Tim had never forgotten his embarrassment, when as a young and inexperienced boatman, he had tried to save time by passing through a bridge hole with the boats tied alongside of each other. He ended up being firmly stuck between the bank and the towpath for four hours. It took three other boats pulling and pushing to finally free him.

Pushing on the large wooden tiller bar, Peggy watched as a crumpled Chinese lantern blew forlornly about in the grip of tangled branches. Grey smoke from a banks man's fire swirled layer upon layer up into the dull sky. He waved his fork, but before Peggy could return the gesture, the wind suddenly changed direction, and he disappeared into the thick smelly gloom. Peggy smiled as she heard him coughing and cursing.

There was mile upon mile of low hills and empty

waterlogged fields, edged with clusters of dense hedgerow, interrupted only by the occasional hamlet, remote farmstead or small industrial building. An intercity train, its livery blurred as it sped by, followed the route of the canal towards London. Old red brick bridges, carrying narrow lanes and cow tracks, some bearing the scars from the constant rub of the horse drawn tow rope. Peggy shivered and pulled her hat down over her ears.

'Yes, another goal.' shouted Dwain, punching the air, as the football thundered into the empty water carrier that they had placed on a chair at the end of the rows of bunks.

'Three nil to me, Zed my man.'

Zed was about to complain that he was over the line when he took the kick, when a very windswept Peggy appeared in the doorway.

'Come on you two, there's a lock coming up.'

'Still say you cheated.' said Zed, hastily putting his buoyancy aid on.

Dwain was laughing as he ran up the steps. 'Just 'cos you can't kick in a straight Line'.

Zed aimed a punch at Dwain's leg but he was too fast. Tim and Peggy had already tied the boats alongside each other ready for the lock.

'Oh, you've surfaced, have you?' shouted Tim, steering the boats into the mooring below the lock.

'Grab that bow line Zed.'

Zed jumped off and ran to the bow of Odin.

Luxted Park was a small flight of four locks. Although not a staircase, they were still very close together. An old woman sat knitting outside the white walled cottage at the side of the lock. She wore a thick green shawl around her shoulders. A mangy looking black dog lay still at her feet. Barney wandered over, sniffed its bum and walked back unimpressed. The dog never moved.

'Maybe it's dead.' chuckled Dwain.

Tim called to her. 'How you doing Mary?'

She nodded.

'Have you seen Smokey recently?'

She shook her head.

'Oh well, I expect we'll see him when we moor for the night.'

She nodded again.

'See you then.' He waved as he steered the boats out of the lock.

'Doesn't say much does she?' said Zed.

Dwain laughed. 'There's some odd people about down 'ere. And who's Smokey?'

'Smokey Joe. He's a sort of tramp, lives in a caravan in the woods. I met 'im a
couple of years ago when I was walking Barney. Tim said 'e was in the army once.'

'Does 'e smell?'

'Spec' so, replied Zed, but then so would you if you were a tramp.'

Suddenly Zed burst into laughter, and started running towards the next lock.

'What do I mean, if you were a tramp? You are a tramp.' he shouted.

'Yeah, whatever Zed.' called Dwain giving chase.

There were no boats coming in the opposite direction, so the boys ran ahead with Barney opening the paddles to empty the lock chambers. This would save them time, as Tim could leave one lock, and drive straight into the next, without waiting for it to be emptied. The light was fading, and as it was only a short distance before they reached Old Mill Lock, Tim decided to call it a day.

The old mill, or what was left of it, stood between

the river Orr and the canal. Once it produced copper sheets for protecting the hulls of wooden warships. Now, only its giant water wheel and chimney remain, dwarfed by the viaduct, which carries the trains across the valley from London to the West Country. This was one of Tim's favourite places to moor for the night, particularly when he had a youth group on board. Across the iron bridge were dense woods ripe for inquisitive young minds to explore, and small shallow pools to fly over on rope swings.

'Ready with the lines.' he shouted, as he pointed the bows towards the bank.

It was Dwain who noticed the sudden movement beyond the treeline, a rustling noise and crackling of dried wood underfoot. His long, brown, double breasted army coat, with shiny buttons merged in well against the carpet of fallen leaves and backcloth of gnarled bark. Beneath the wide rimmed leather hat, adorned with a feather plucked from a recently deceased pheasant, was a jolly round face that had been whipped by the winds of time. His fulsome grey beard hung majestically from his chin like a Scotsman's sporran.

'Is that you Tim?' he called stepping from the wood onto the towpath.

Tim was on his knees turning Odin's grease gland, and only his backside was visible to Smokey.

'It's me Smokey.' he replied straightening up.

Smokey laughed. 'I thought I recognised that bum.'

Barney was sniffing at his coat pocket.

'He can smell the chicken I had last night.'

Tim didn't dare ask where it came from.

'This is Zed and Dwain.' said Tim introducing the boys, 'they're from London.'

Smokey screwed up his face. 'London, horrible place, too many miserable people, and too much traffic.'

The boys nodded in agreement.

Peggy stuck her head out of the side hatch. "Cup of tea Smokey?'

'Just the job, my love. Could murder a brew.'

'I met you before," said Zed suddenly.

Smokey took a step back and looked him up and down 'You did? Where was that then?'

'Ere, two years ago, when I was walking Barney.'

He laughed, 'two years. Roamed many a path since then.'

Dwain whispered to Zed, ''E don't smell.'

Zed nudged him. 'Shut up.'

Tim took a silver hip flask from his jacket pocket and poured some of the contents into their mugs. 'That'll warm the cockles, Smokey.'

Zed was just about to ask what the cockles were when Peggy called them down below to help prepare dinner.

'I expect Smokey will stay for a meal.' she said, throwing a bag of potatoes at the boys. 'Peel them this time, don't demolish them.'

The boys resigned themselves to their fate, there was no escape this time.

A large bowl of Peggy's Stampot and Herfstbock Dutch stew with plump suet dumplings, eaten next to a roaring fire. Their young minds seduced by the hypnotic rhythm of the dancing flames. Another log gets thrown from a dark corner sending sparks flying upwards into the star littered sky.

'You have heard of the Vikings, haven't you?' asked Smokey poking a long stick into the red embers.

Dwain nodded; Zed wasn't quite so sure.

Dwain had asked Tim where the names Thor and Odin had come from.

Smokey stroked his long beard. Thor, he said, was the son of Odin, the Viking god of thunder, and the strongest of all the gods. His mother Jord was the earth goddess.

'Cool.' said Dwain, 'that's some parents.'

'So, it's 'im that makes the thunder?' asked Zed.

'That's what the Vikings believed, and if a Viking warrior died clutching his
sword, then he would go to the feast hall at Valhalla.'

'What's that? Some sort of heaven?' asked Dwain.
Smokey smiled. 'You could say that.'

Peggy handed the boys two cups of steaming hot chocolate. Tim and Smokey were finishing of the last off the contents of Tim's flask.

'What's yer cockles?' asked Zed suddenly.

'Yer what?' queried Tim.

Zed repeated the question. 'Yer cockles. Earlier you said, this would warm yer cockles.'

The men both laughed.

'It's just a figure of speech Zed, it means to warm up your heart.'

'Right.' said Zed, a little disappointed that he hadn't discovered a new part of his anatomy.

Smokey stood up and walked slowly round the fire, Barney followed. Occasionally he would stop to kick a burning log back into the fire.

'You do know that us men of the road have our own sort of Valhalla, where we go when we shuffle off this earth. Oh yes, we don't go to any ordinary heaven.'

Tim laughed out loud. 'Or hell.'

'Take no notice of disbelievers.' said Smokey.

'Where do you go then?' asked Dwain.

'Skidledoor.' shouted Smokey, raising his arms skyward, 'heaven of the tramps.'

Zed asked if you 'ave to be holding something to get there?'

Smokey looked puzzled, 'What do you mean holding something?

'Well, you said the Vikings only went to Valhalla if

65

they were holding a sword.'

'Ah, I see what you mean.' said Smokey.

Zed persisted. 'So, what do you have to hold?'

Before Smokey could answer, Tim shouted out, 'a stolen chicken.'

'Oh, very funny.' said Smokey.

'You don't nick chickens do yer?' asked Dwain.

Smokey gave Tim a wry smile. 'Good grief, no boy. I wouldn't go to Skidledoor if I did that.'

'Come on you two, say goodnight.' said Peggy, 'we've got an early start in the morning'

'Ta ta.' shouted Smokey. See you again, and don't stay in that London too long, it'll fry yer brain'.

Tim and Smokey had known each other a long time. Tim had first met Joseph, as he was known then, when he came to Tiddledurn, from his home in Birmingham, to spend the summer with his uncle. He was eleven and Tim eighteen, and although Tim was older, they had struck up a friendship.

Tim taught him how to fish and handle a narrowboat. Like Zed he came every Easter and summer holiday until he joined the army at eighteen. It would be many years before Tim and Smokey met again. They sat round the fire reminiscing until the early hours of the morning, then, as the red embers dulled Smokey Joe disappeared back into the dark woods.

Dwain opened one bleary eye. 'You awake Zed?'

He groaned. 'Not really what time is it?'

Dwain checked his phone. 'Ten to eight.'

Zed groaned again and rolled over.

Hearing their voices Barney ran through the boat and jumped onto Zed's bunk, slapping him in the ear with his muddy paw.

'Ah, get off you fat dog.' he shouted.

Barney took no notice.

'The sun is a shining to welcome the day, hey ho come to the fair.' sang Tim loudly, whilst bashing a ladle on to the bottom of a saucepan.

'Go away.' called Zed pulling the sleeping bag up over his head.

'Time and Tide..........'

'Wait for no one.' shouted Dwain rolling from his bunk.

Tim banged the pot nearer to Zed's head. 'Well done young Dwain, you're learning.'

'Alright, I'm getting up.' shouted Zed, pushing Barney off the bunk.

'Breakfast in ten minutes.' called Peggy, stirring a large pot of porridge.

The boys quickly showered and sat at the long table that usually accommodated twelve people. As Peggy served their porridge, Tim crept up behind them and placed two big Easter Eggs on the table in front of them. 'Happy Easter.' he said putting his large arms around their shoulders.

'Thanks Tim, thanks Peggy.' shouted the boys. Zed was just about to open his egg when Peggy interrupted. 'Breakfast first I think young man.'

Tim had tidied the fire pit at the edge of the woods, and was carrying out the engine checks on Odin. The boys, with Barney, had made Old Mill Lock ready. They had raced to see who could raise the paddles the quickest. Zed won, just.

Henry, the heron, stood motionless as unsuspecting shiny silhouettes flashed by beneath the surface. A pair of swans, smaller than Sammy and Sheena, glided gracefully towards the bank in search of an early breakfast.

The canal narrowed after the lock. Standing next to

Tim and Barney, Zed steered Odin while Peggy and Dwain followed on Thor.

'We'll be at Shimington Tunnel soon.' said Peggy.
Zed told Dwain that it was really long. 'It's over a mile and very dark.'

'Ow did the boats get through when horses pulled 'em?' asked Dwain.
Peggy explained that they had to be legged through the tunnel, and the horse would be taken over the hill to meet the boat on the other side.

'What's legging?' asked Dwain.

'One person would lie on their back on a plank of wood, with their legs over the side of the boat and their feet on the wall of the tunnel. The same thing would happen on the other side of the boat with another person.

Lying flat like that, they would push their feet against the tunnel wall and do a sideways walk that would pull the boat along with them.

'That sounds like 'ard work, I'm glad we got an engine.' laughed Dwain.
Tim waved and reduced the speed to slow the boats down.

'Here we are.' said Peggy, Shimington Tunnel.'
After they had moored both the boats up to the bank Zed told Peggy that his uncle Darren had rung him again.

'Ignore him," said Peggy, 'although I will ring your gran this afternoon, to see if   she knows why he wants to see you.'
The boys and Barney ran ahead to peer into the mouth of the dark tunnel.

'A cup of tea I think, before we go through there.' said Peggy.

Good Idea.' replied Tim, checking that the headlights on the front of the boats worked.

CHAPTER SIX

The fox's lair

In a wet field on the outskirts of the town of Taunton in Somerset, De Vito's travelling circus and fairground were in hibernation. Giant towing lorries were parked idly in a row, their powerful engines stilled until the spring. The bright crimson livery tarnished and dulled by the winter onslaught. Mobile homes of all shapes and sizes were arranged nose to tail in a wide circle, as if defending the community against an unseen enemy. The long trailers stored all the equipment needed to transform an ordinary town or village green into a magic place of fun and laughter.

Darren, Zed's uncle, was employed at the circus as a ganger and along with other ganger's his job was to hump, erect and dismantle. It was heavy routine work which demanded much muscle but little thought, this suited Darren. Not that he was stupid, far from it. Darren was a chancer, and as cunning as a fox.

It was into this world that Gran had sent Zed, after he had been excluded from his junior school and his mother was sent to prison. Her intentions were good, wanting to get him away from London, where he was getting into bad company. She had no idea his uncle would neglect him. Zed wasn't strong enough to hump, so he spent his time making tea for the gangers, picking up litter, and selling programmes, whilst living on a diet of hot dogs and candy floss. It was while being sold a programme by Zed, that Peggy and Tim had first seen him when the circus visited Tiddledurn two years ago.

Darren's small shabby caravan was parked in the corner of the field outside the main circle of smart mobile homes. Like the old van that towed it, there were patches of rust and flaking paintwork. He shared it with another ganger, a man of similar age and outlook. Lee White, was, like Darren, a drifter, meaning he drifted in and out of trouble. Both had been guests of Her Majesty's Prisons. Lee had joined the circus last summer when it had come to the green at Tiddledurn, as it did every year. His last job, clearing undergrowth in a wood, had ended with the sudden death of the land owner, and albeit a casual role, he was sorry to leave as he liked working outside in the fresh air. It was in the village pub one evening that he had met Zed's uncle Darren, who had told him of the ganger vacancy at the circus. Lee applied, got the job, and moved in to Darren's caravan. The circus moved on, and them with it, and then one night deep in the fox's lair, a chance remark by Lee, led to a cunning plan being hatched.

There was a slither of moon the night that Rocket Ron decided to stake out the farmhouse at Muckle Farm. He checked his watch. If he was coming it wouldn't be long now. Ron had suspected that someone was squatting at the farmhouse, ever since finding the remains of a fire in the kitchen when walking Frankie and Freddie. Ron reckoned he was up to no good, particularly as some of the boats moored alongside the towpath had been broken into recently. Peering from behind the barn door, across the yard from the farmhouse, he watched as the prowling fox came close to where he was standing. He stopped, his brown, glassy eyes reflecting in the moon's white light, then, sniffing the air he turned and disappeared into the darkness.

There was a light, dim at first somewhere just beyond the gate which hung on one rusty hinge. Ron pressed his back to the door. He shivered as the cold night wind rattled round the loose corrugated roof of the barn. His heart was racing now, and although feeling cold, beads of sweat were breaking on his brow. Slow heavy footsteps pressed down against the gravelled surface. Then the torch light died.

The man had stopped, and was standing very quiet and still in the middle of the farmyard. Ron hardly dared to breath. Had he heard him? Did he suspect something? A striking match. Then a pencil thin red glow that flared and dimmed, flared and dimmed. Bats flew low from the rafters of the barn, skimming close to Ron's head.

He jumped knocking over an old wooden crate that was standing on the floor next to him. Ron waited, but the man had heard nothing. His heart was beating even faster. Was he reading too much into this? After all the guy could just be homeless and looking for shelter. Why otherwise would anyone stay in a cold, deserted farmhouse? Thoughts were racing round Ron's head. What would he do if the man saw him? He was too old to run away, and he couldn't say he was walking Frankie and Freddie as he had left them on the boat. He wished he had brought them though, particularly Freddie as he was a vicious little devil.

The pencil thin, red glow fell to the ground and was extinguished. The torch light was switched on. Ron watched as the man moved into the farmhouse. He was tall, and carried a bag over his shoulder. Ron waited for a while in case he came out again. A weak light shone from beyond the tattered curtains of the kitchen window. Ron carefully edged his way around the perimeter of the yard until he was standing next to the farmhouse. Ducking down, he crawled under the darkened first window, before reaching the porch. From here he could lean across and see through the kitchen window.

On the table stood a hurricane lamp flickering in the draught. The man was younger than Ron expected. His long brown hair reached down to his shoulders, although partly hidden by a woollen hat. He opened a tin of baked beans, then drank from a can of coke, before throwing it across the room. Unzipping his blue anorak, he took out a long hunting knife, stabbing it down hard into the wooden kitchen table, then from his ruck- sack came a sleeping bag and hand axe, which he slammed into the table next to the quivering knife.

Ron moved quickly away from the kitchen window as the man walked across the room to where the cold fireplace was. Suddenly the kitchen door opened, and he came out into the porch holding the hand axe. Ron froze. He could hear his heavy breathing on the other side of the wooden porch wall. There was a hard thud as an axe was driven into a log, then another, a pause, then a cracking sound as the wood split open. Ron's hands and legs were shaking, a mixture of cold and fear. Another thud, and more cracking wood. He said something to himself, but Ron couldn't make out what. Kicking the door open he carried the logs inside. Ron breathed a sigh of relief. It had been nearly three hours and his legs hurt like hell. Ducking down he crawled under the kitchen window and walked carefully across the darkened yard. He didn't need a torch; he knew the terrain like the back of his hand. After going through the gate which hung on the rusty hinge, he went down the slope and onto the towpath towards his boat. Tomorrow he would return.

They met in Fran's greasy spoon café in a back street of Melbury. One had arrived by train, the other by bus from Tiddledurn. Both ordered the Big Breakfast from the menu.

One of them ate much quicker than the other, having lived on tinned rice and baked beans for a week. He looked scruffy and unkempt, keeping his blue anorak on throughout, even though it was warm inside the café.

"Ow did yer get on?' asked the one wearing the donkey jacket.

Wiping his plate with a piece of bread, he replied that he knew her name and where she lived.

'Ave yer seen her.'

'Yeah, on the towpath, it's definitely 'er.'

'She didn't recognise yer?'

Laughing, he replied. 'No, I hid behind a tree. 'Ow did you get on with yer nephew?'

'Nothing, won't even answer me calls.'

'So, what now?'

He took a mouthful of tea from a large white mug. 'We 'gotta find out where she's stashed the gear.'

'Is there any way you could get in for a look round?'

He shook his head. 'No way mate, she always locks up when she goes out.

Anyway, I doubt the gears on the boat.'

The man with the donkey jacket stirred more sugar into his tea. 'Maybe.'

'So 'ow do we find out?'

He smiled. 'Watch and wait my friend, watch and wait.'

'It's all right for you Darren, I'm the one freezing every night in that old farmhouse.'

'Think of the bonus mate, it'll be worth it.'

'I 'ope so, I need the dosh.'

Darren stood up. 'I gotta get back. Make sure yer phone's on. I'll ring yer when I 've 'ad time to think. Take this it should keep you going.' He handed over an envelope with £50 in it.

'They are keeping me job open?'

'Course.' He laughed. 'They think yer visiting yer dying gran in Ireland.

Oh, by the way, I've found a bloke to fence the gear.' he said putting on his donkey jacket. Outside they punched

73

fists. 'Laters.' called the man in the blue anorak as they parted company from each other.

Rocket Ron lifted his bike from the roof of his narrowboat. Leaning it against a tree, he put Frankie and Freddie in the wooden box that was secured over the rear mudguard. Freddie had other plans though, jumping down and scampering quickly up the grassy bank before Ron could catch him.

'Come back here, you pesky rodent.' shouted Ron, throwing a stick at him.

Freddie sat defiantly at the top of the slope.

'Stay there then, I hope a passing sparrow hawk has you for lunch.'

Ron hadn't gone too far when Freddie came running after him. Scooping up the errant ferret, he dropped him in the box with Frankie. He cursed the ruts in the towpath that nearly pitched him into the canal. It wouldn't be the first time he had taken a swim.

Jean didn't hear the shop door open. She was out the back, on her knees trying to prize a half dead mouse from the cat's jaws.

'Allo, anybody there?' he shouted urgently. The man in a blue anorak was pressing a dirty, blood-soaked cloth to his left hand.

'You sell plasters?' he asked abruptly.

'What have you done?' asked Jean.

'Cut it chopping wood.' he replied, removing the cloth from his hand so she could see. There was a deep jagged gash in his forefinger. Jean noticed he had the word 'LOVE' tattooed in blue across his nicotine stained fingers.

'You will need to have that stitched.' she said, placing a box of plasters on the counter.

'Got no time for that.' he said, fumbling to open

74

them. He dropped the box onto the floor.

'Would you like me to do it?' Jean asked.
The man nodded. 'Thanks.'

Jean had just peeled the back from the large plaster when the door opened and Frankie and Freddie came scampering in to the shop. The man looked startled. Freddie made straight for the little droplets of blood on the floor.

'Get away from that.' damn vampires," shouted Ron, giving Freddie a swift kick.

'Nasty cut mate.' said Ron, looking at the man's hand.

The man turned to face him, 'I'll be more careful with the axe next time.'

Ron realised straight away that he was talking to the man who was squatting at Muckle Farm, the man he had been watching, and who he suspected was up to no good.

'You live local mate?' asked Ron, knowing full well he didn't.

'I'm just passing through.'

'Oh right.' answered Ron. 'Where you headed for then?'

The man ignored him and turned back to Jean 'Could I get some groceries while I'm 'ere please.'

'Course love. Tell me what do you need.'

Once the man had left the shop Ron asked Jean if she knew who he was.

'I've never seen him before.' replied Jean, packing Ron's groceries into a bag.

'He's squatting up at Muckle Farm.' said Ron, 'I've been watching him.'

'What do mean, watching him?'

'Like I said, I've been watching him come and go, and I know he's up to something.'

Jean laughed. 'You've been reading too much Sherlock
75

Holmes, if you think it's suspicious then why don't you call PC Thomas?'

Ron shook his head. 'What's the point? I can't prove anything.'

'Exactly.' said Jean throwing the ferrets a piece of out of date ham.

She paused. 'unless.'

'Unless what?' asked Ron.

'The other day Peggy was telling me that a man stopped Zed and Dwain on the towpath.'

Ron was getting impatient. 'What did he want?'

'Whether they knew Coote's Wood, and the woman who used to visit him there.'

'What, you mean Rose?'

Jean gestured with her hands. Well who else can it be?'

'What did the boys say?'

'That they didn't know anything.'

Ron thought for a moment. 'I'll ring Peggy later, see if the boys can describe him.'

'But what could he possibly want with Rose?' asked Jean.

'I don't know, but we need to find out.'

Ron was getting onto his bike when Jean came to the door.

'There was one other thing Ron, he knew Zed's name.'

CHAPTER SEVEN

Bringing the boats back

Shimington tunnel to Tiddledurn.

Tim turned on the powerful headlight that was mounted on the front of Odin.

     'Let go, and shove off.' he shouted to Zed who was

standing ready at the bow of the boat.

Zed gave a big push, then jumped on as the boat moved away from the bank. Peggy and Dwain did the same with Thor. Because they were going through the narrow tunnel Tim had left Thor tied astern, so it could be towed by Odin. As Odin's bow pierced the blackness at the mouth of the tunnel, the wide beam from its headlight illuminated the fungi strewn brickwork. Barney wasn't happy as he had been put down below in Tim's cabin, just in case he fell overboard.

'This is creepy.' said Dwain pulling his hood up tight over his head. 'What 'appens if something comes the other way?"

'Two boats can pass each other, but it's very tight.' answered Peggy, dodging a steam of water that was falling from an overhead ventilation shaft.

Dwain watched behind as the daylight at the entrance to the tunnel slowly eclipsed, before disappearing altogether, then total darkness. He hung on tightly to the side rail.

'How would you fancy legging through here then?' Peggy asked.

Dwain laughed. 'I wouldn't. Too much like 'ard work.'

'Boys of your age had to do it though.'

'They must 'ave been tough kids.'

Peggy nodded. 'They were, it was a hard life.' said Peggy, especially for the children.'

'Didn't they 'ave to go to school then?'

'Well no, they couldn't, they were always on the move.'

Dwain laughed. 'That sounds alright to me.'

Zed was steering Odin. Tim had passed him the tiller bar while he went down into his stern cabin. He didn't need anything, but wanted to give Zed the space and confidence to steer on his own. Barney was asleep on

Tim's bed. He opened one eye and begrudgingly wagged the end of his tail.

'Are you sulking, daft dog?' said Tim poking him with his finger.

Barney ignored him, closed his eye and went back to sleep.

'You alright Zed?' he called

'I would be if I could see where I'm going.'

Tim laughed. 'Just don't make any sudden sharp turns.'

'Very funny.'

Peggy was telling Dwain how the tunnel was built in 1796 by men called 'navvies', which was short for navigator.

'It must 'ave taken a long time to build.' said Dwain.

'It did.' she replied. 'Don't forget, all the earth and rocks had to be dug out by hand using only a shovel and pickaxe. It was back breaking work, and many of them were injured and killed.'

They moved slowly through the tunnel occasionally bumping into the uneven walls. A little while later, and a bit further on, they saw a tiny glare of sunlight slowly grow as they came to the end. One of Harry Martin's hire boats was coming in to the tunnel. Tim waved as they passed by. 'Have a good time.' he shouted over the noise of the engine. Zed turned off the headlight, then pressed the throttle forward to increase the speed of the boats.

'Well done boy.' said Tim, punching him lightly on the arm, 'good bit of steering.' Zed stood a little bit taller after that compliment.

Tim was the only father figure he had ever known, he loved and respected him, and Peggy of course, not that he would ever tell Tim that, as he didn't do 'Mush' as he called it.

'Is that your phone ringing Peg?' asked Dwain.

Peggy took off her gloves and fumbled in her deep pocket. 'Hello.'

'It's Rocket Ron.' she said to Dwain. 'Can you hold keep the boat straight?'

They skirted around the new golf course where the old manor house once stood, and horses came to the water's edge to drink.

'Can't see the point.' said Tim, 'hitting a ball then walking half a mile to find it.'

Zed laughed.

A sharp left-hand bend tested Zed's steering skills, leaning hard over on the tiller bar, he tweaked the throttle just enough to bring the nose round, without hitting the bank.

'Good man," said Tim, 'I'll be able to retire soon.'

Peggy tooted Thor's horn, and gave him a thumbs up.

'I need a brew," said Tim, 'we'll moor at Lido Park, it's not far now.'

There were no mooring rings, so they banged in long metal spikes with a club hammer to hold the lines. Peggy told the boys that Rocket Ron had phoned, and could they remember what the man they had met on the towpath was wearing.'

'Has 'e seen 'im then? said Zed.

'Possibly.' replied Peggy, 'and it's 'He', and 'Him', with an H.'

'He 'ad long 'air, I fink it was brown.' said Dwain.

Peggy shook her head, 'I do try.'

The boys smiled at each other.

Zed added. 'And 'e hadn't shaved.'

'What about his jacket and trousers?'

'It was one of those anorak things.' said Zed.

Peggy asked if they could remember the colour.

'Blue.' said Dwain, 'light blue.'

Zed nodded in agreement.

'OK, I'll ring him and let him know. Now, who would like a sandwich?'

The boys ate their sandwiches sitting on a wooden bench dedicated to an 'Arthur Reeves' who had died in June 2015, and 'Loved This Place'.

'Wonder what yer 'gotta do to 'ave a seat named after yer?' asked Zed.

'Dunno.' replied Dwain, 'just sit here long enough I s'pose.'

Zed chuckled. 'Or die,'

'What's a Lido?' asked Dwain.

'It's what they call an outdoor swimming pool.'

'Don't fancy that, be too cold," said Dwain, as the thought of it made him shiver.

Zed laughed and threw the last of his sandwich at some passing ducks.

'They only use it in the summer, you dipstick.'

There were happy memories for Zed here. They had moored at Lido Park two years ago, when they were taking Kingfisher, the boat Zed stowed away on, back to Boswell's Yard. Peggy had gone for one of her long walks. Tim had set up the rods and shown Zed how to catch a fish. Not that they did, but it didn't matter. Just the two of them sitting quietly together, on the bank of the canal, in that moment, was something Zed would never forget.

Peggy had an affinity for this place. She would cross over the bridge which led to the park, then walk up the steep hill to the Lido. Once through the big iron gates, she would cross the road that ran through the village where she had lived as a girl. It was a small cemetery, hidden behind a tall red brick wall. The small grave, underneath the branches of an old oak tree, was marked by a plain white headstone, with the inscription 'David Hickman aged five days.' It was Peggy's son.

Peggy had met Karl, David's dad, when he was

working at the circus which came every year to the park with the Lido. They were both eighteen. Peggy had become pregnant. The circus had moved on and with it, Karl. This was Peggy's secret. Only her parents had known about it and they were no longer alive.

It was early afternoon by the time they left Lido Park. Dwain and Zed were sitting on the narrow board that ran from bow to stern along the top of the canvas roof on Odin. A pair of dark Chinook helicopters flew in low from a distant ridge, their twin rotor blades violently threshing the still air. The boys could see the pilots in their cockpits, and waved as the passed overhead. Banking to starboard they circled round again before disappearing across the hills towards the plains beyond. Occasional loud, dull thuds echoed along the canal as tanks and artillery played war games on the army ranges.

The land was climbing gently, flat, wet fields giving way to undulating terrain and thick woods, as the canal crept steadily into the Vale of Yalding. Tim slowed down as they passed by a long line of moored boats, wide beams, fibre glass cruisers and narrowboats. At the end stood the Yalding Boat Club house, with deck chairs arranged on a small wooden veranda.

The building had seen better days. A ripped flag hung limply above the roof without the breeze to lift it away from the pole. The grounds were surrounded by a tall metal fence topped with rusty barbed wire, flaked with pieces of skin and torn clothing. Boaters were always forgetting their gate key.

Tim and Peggy rarely came here. They didn't fit in with the social order which was dictated by those with electricity, and those without, and those with bow thrusters and those without. Tim often said that the owners fell into the same categories as the boats, both physically and psychologically; narrow, wide, and small, and some were certainly cruisers.

On the opposite side of the canal to the Boat Club was what remained of the old flour mill, which for the last two weeks had been slowly devoured by huge, quasi – prehistoric metal jaws attached to the end of a long hydraulic arm. From the other end of the site came a loud chomping and gnawing, as another beast like machine gorged on live trees which had been felled to quench its insatiable appetite. It then puked them out into piles of lifeless chippings to be carted away and made into coffins.

'Criminal.' Tim said to Barney, 'another landmark gone, probably turn it into another wretched housing estate.' Barney looked up but didn't answer him.

Peggy had phoned Rocket Ron back. Now he knew for sure that the man he had spoken to in Jean's shop, was the same one who had questioned Zed and Dwain on the towpath. But what was he up to? And why was he interested in Rose's visits to old Mr Coote? There was no point in asking Rose, Peggy had already done that. He would have to wait and watch him, until he revealed his hand, then with enough evidence he could alert PC Thomas, and maybe prevent a crime.
He chuckled to himself, 'I suppose I could always ask him. What do you think Freddie?'

Freddie had climbed onto his shoulder and was nibbling his ear.

'Maybe that's not such a good idea, he might turn nasty.'
He dropped Freddie onto the floor with Frankie, who was just about to climb up his trouser leg.

'I suppose you two want your dinner. Come on then, let's see if we can find a nice pair of fresh mice.'

Wills, Jean's tom cat at the shop, kept Freddie and Frankie supplied with freshly killed mice, and occasionally a special treat of a juicy rat or squirrel. Ron would resume his stake out at Muckle Farm tonight, and every night until he found out what the man was up to.

Lee pushed a wedge of white crusty bread around his plate, finishing off the last of one of Fran's Big Breakfasts. They were meeting again in the greasy spoon café in Melbury so Darren could reveal his master plan.

'She goes out for a fair bit on a Thursday.' We could break in then.' said Lee.

Darren slurped from a large mug of tea. 'Yeah, but if we turn the place over and find

nothing we're stuffed, she'll call the law, and move the gear.'

'Like I said before, maybe it's not there.' said Lee.

Darren shook his head. 'It's there alright, I can't see the old bird putting it in a bank.'

'So, what do we do then Darren?'

He laughed. 'We go in when she's there, and we encourage her to tell us where it is. Simple.'

'And what if she don't?' asked Lee.

Darren picked up a plastic ketchup bottle and gave it a hard squeeze. '

Then we encourage 'er some more.' he laughed.

Lee produced a piece of grubby paper from his pocket and handed it to Darren. It was a record of Rose's movements for the last week. Darren studied the creased list.

'She don't go out much does she, and always 'ome by four in the afternoon.'

Lee nodded. 'Yeah that's right.'

'What about visitors?'

'The only person I saw, was the old bloke with the ferrets, and 'e always came in the morning.'

Darren thought for a moment. 'Perfect.' he said, 'it'll be nice and quiet. We'll pay 'er a visit next week.'

'So, what do I do now?' asked Lee.

Darren stood up to leave. 'You might as well come back to the circus with me, you can tell 'em yer gran got better.' he chuckled.

'Or pegged it.' laughed Lee, who was just glad he didn't have to spend another night squatting at Muckle Farm.

Feeling pleased with themselves they caught the train back to Taunton where De'Vito's Circus was resting for the winter.

It is said that the robbers, Black Jack and One-legged Laura, stopped at the Crown Tavern in the vale before riding to Melbury Lock to hold up and rob passing boatman. Over one hundred years later it was still being frequented by some rather dubious characters. The Emerson brothers, Ben and Jimmy, were well known on the cut for their shady activities, such as acquiring and selling boat equipment before the true owner realised it had gone.

Ben waved and shouted something to Tim as the boats drew level with the pub garden where they were both sitting. Tim couldn't hear what he was saying, so he signalled to Peggy and put the boat's engine into neutral.

Ben shouted again. 'Alright Tim? Got some nice batteries if yer interested, good price to you.'

Tim laughed. 'No thanks mate, I'm alright.'

'What about you Peg? called Jimmy. 'Got some cheap coal and logs.'

Peggy waved and shook her head. 'Got plenty Jimmy, thanks all the same.'

Zed and Dwain slid on their bottoms back along the narrow plank to where Tim was standing on the stern. 'Who were they?' asked Zed.

'Local villains. They'd get on well with your uncle Darren.'

Tim nudged the stern of Odin against the bank so Dwain could run back and join Peggy on Thor.

'So, are you enjoying yourself?' she asked Dwain.

'It's great, Zed's really lucky 'aving you two.'

'Well I suppose it was meant to be.' said Peggy. 'If we hadn't gone to the circus that day we would never had met him.'

'It took some guts to run away from there.' said Dwain.

Peggy laughed. 'The little devil ran away twice. When we got Kingfisher back to Boswell's Yard, we had arranged for Zed to stay the night with Janice Phillips, she teaches at the village school. Her husband was going to take him back to London the next day. But Zed had other ideas and left in the middle of the night.'

'Where did he go?' asked Dwain.

Peggy smiled. 'We eventually found him on 'Odin.'

'Bet he was in trouble.'

Peggy shook her head. 'No, we were just happy that we found him safe.'

'So how come 'e stayed for the 'olidays? asked Dwain.

'Well, I spoke to his gran, and we both agreed that if we forced him to go back to London, he might run away again, and as the school holidays were coming up it seemed sensible for him to stay with us.'

'But 'e wasn't in school.'

'He wasn't, so we made a deal. Janice would try to get him back into school in London and he could continue to come down here so long as he worked hard at school'.

'Wow," said Dwain, 'that's really cool.'

'Well it seems to have worked.' said Peggy, 'and the last thing any of us want is for him to end up like his dreadful Uncle Darren.'

Tim waved to Peggy to signal that he was slowing the boats down.

'We're at the Haddon Aqueduct.' said Peggy.
The stretch leading to the aqueduct was very crowded. Canoes and kayaks were criss crossing the canal, bumping into the bank and colliding with each other.
Tim said it was like Waterborne dodgem cars. The old coal wharf had been converted into a café, which also hired out cycles, canoes and kayaks. Haddon Aqueduct was always busy. As well as those hiring boats from the wharf, many visited to walk along the river which ran underneath the aqueduct. Gongoozlers came to watch the boats and their skippers and crews, particularly when they were turning their boats around in the Winding Hole. This is the name given to a place on the canal where boats can turn around. Narrowboats do not like windy weather. This can make turning them around much harder, but good fun for the Gongoozlers. Tim and Peggy would not be creating any entertainment for them as they steered the boats round the bend and onto the aqueduct. The boys looked over the sides into the valley below where the river and road ran adjacent to one another. Dwain laughed as a platoon of Canada geese, their heads bobbing in unison floated by in an orderly line, just like soldiers. One of Harry Martin's hire boats was waiting to enter the aqueduct after Odin and Thor had passed through.
'It's Kingfisher.' shouted Zed, waving to get Dwain's attention.
'What's he saying? 'asked Peggy.
''E said the boat up ahead is Kingfisher.'
Peggy told Dwain that Zed has a special affinity with that boat.
'A special what?' asked Dwain.
'Affinity, love. It means a connection or fondness.'
'Yeah, s'pose he does, that's 'ow he met you two.'
Peggy nodded, 'that's right love.'

Tim lent on the tiller bar as they turned into the sharp right-hand bend at the end of the aqueduct. On the other side of the horse bridge a lone fisherman sat hunched over his rod. His concentration was so focused on his little orange float that he failed to see or hear the boats coming. Tim hadn't seen him either, for he was completely dressed in green camouflage, which merged in with the long grass at the edge of the canal. Odin's bow hit the small float and line, dragging the rod from its stand where it had been resting. Startled from his meditation, the fisherman jumped up from his seat, and tried to catch the rod before it fell into the water. But it was too late.

'Oi, you've caught my line.' he shouted angrily.

'Sorry mate.' called Tim, 'I didn't see you there.'

He waved to Peggy to indicate that he was stopping, then asked Zed to stand by with the boathook to recover the rod. Zed had trouble seeing it at first, then suddenly it bobbed up from under the bow of the boat. He eventually managed to get the hook between the line and the rod and pull it out of the water. Tim nudged the boat into the bank so Zed could hand it back to the unhappy fisherman.

As Odin reversed away from the bank Zed joked to him that he could say he caught a boat. He didn't answer and disappeared into his little igloo shaped tent.

''E wasn't very 'appy.' said Zed.

Tim laughed. 'Woke him up though, didn't it?'

The outskirts of Melbury town were pushing further and further into the surrounding countryside. They passed the small airfield where Tim came as a child to watch the planes taking off and landing. Now only the car park remained, surrounded by giant soulless buildings that made up the new industrial estate.

Peggy passed the tiller bar to Dwain while she went down into her cabin to make a cup of tea. She returned with a bag of her favourite jelly babies. '

'Right young Dwain, let's play a little game. You up for it?'

'Go for it Peg.' he said eyeing the sweets.

She laughed. 'A jelly baby for each right answer.'

'He nodded, 'ok.'

'What's the front of the boat called?'

He answered straight away. 'The bow.'

'Back of the boat?'

'Stern.'

She handed him two jelly babies. 'Well done.'

'The right-hand side of the boat looking from the stern?'

He thought for a moment, 'starboard.'

'Very good. The left-hand side of the boat?'

He laughed. 'It's got to be port.'

She handed him two more of the sweets.

'Right, last two, what do we wind the paddles up with?'

'You mean that metal 'fing?'

'Yes, what's it called?'

He banged his hand on the tiller bar. A wind, something.'

She waved a jelly baby in front of him, 'nearly.'

'Windmass.'he shouted.

Peggy laughed. 'Near enough.' 'It's windlass.'

Dwain grabbed the jelly baby.

'Fenders.' she asked.

'Fenders.' he repeated, thinking aloud, 'fenders, oh I know, the things that 'ang on the side of the boat to protect it from being damaged.'

She handed him the last jelly baby. 'Well done. 'she said.

They went under a bridge, where the busy main road to Melbury passed overhead and then around a very sharp left-hand bend and into a wide part of the canal where boats could turn around. Peggy asked Dwain if he could remember the name of the turning point. He could, and said it was a Winding Hole. Peggy was impressed and gave him another jelly baby.

Boats were moored both sides of the canal leading to Melbury Lock. Most were residential moorings with small gardens. Some had lots of flowers with tidy lawns, while others had vegetable plots with wooden sheds where they kept their tools and gardening equipment. Tim slowed down because moored boaters did get upset if passing boats went too fast, as the wash made their boat rock and bang against the side of the bank. Tim and Peggy still hadn't roped Odin alongside 'Thor'.

They would need to do this before they could enter the lock, luckily there was room to moor one boat behind the other. Tim asked the boys to empty the lock while he and Peggy got the boats ready. Barney hadn't been off the boat for some time and shot into the cricket field to relieve himself.

'Do yer reckon that's the tree Black Jack used to climb into?' said Zed.

'I reckon so, it's the tallest one there, you could see for miles.' said Dwain pushing open the lock gate.

'Who was the other ghost Rose told us about?' asked Zed. 'She said he'd be watching us.'

Dwain thought for a moment, 'Albert Wilks, the lock keeper.'

'Maybe we'll see 'im.'

'Doubt it.' said Dwain, 'they only come out at night when nobody's about to see 'em.'

Tim and Peggy steered the boats into the lock, and the boys shut the gates.

'Race "yer.' shouted Zed, as they ran to the other end of the lock.

They put their windlasses on to the spindle and turned as fast as they could go. Dwain won.

90

It was only a short distance from Melbury Lock to Tim's cottage at Tiddledurn, where Odin and Thor had their moorings. They rounded the bend by the stables, passing under the bridge which carried the intercity trains. Snowdrops carpeted the margins of the woods, where bluebells grow in the spring, and Peggy loves to visit.

A chilled dusk had settled over Jean's long garden. Tim glided the boats alongside the small wooden jetty so Peggy and Barney could jump off. Barney needed to pee, and she needed some pasta. Tim and Peggy hated the stuff but the boys liked it. Zed ran back to join Dwain on the stern of Thor. He would steer the short distance left before they reached their home moorings. Wills, Jean's black tomcat, was lying sprawled on a wooden bench, a half dead field mouse between his paws. He hissed when Barney came too close.

As they rounded the last bend on their journey, Tim signalled to Zed to indicate that he was slowing down. As the towrope slackened, he untied it from the stern of Odin. Zed pointed Thor's bow to the port side of Odin. Tim then walked along the gunwales holding the line. When both boats were level with each other Tim tied Thor's bowline to the front of Odin, Zed did the same with the stern line. With both boats lashed tightly together Tim could steer the boats onto the moorings.

Peggy left Jean's shop and walked slowly along the towpath towards Tim's cottage. Barney ran ahead, he was glad to be off the boat. She was thinking about the boys, and how well they got on with each other. She liked Dwain; it was good for Zed to have someone of his own age when he stayed with them. The earlier phone call with Zed's gran Betty, was worrying her. Why was Darren, Zed's uncle, so insistent on being given Zed's mobile number? He obviously didn't care about him, that's why Zed ran away in the first place. So why the sudden interest? What was he up to? Across the fields the street lights from the Melbury Road projected an orange glow high into the dark sky.

Two kayaks, with little white lights mounted on their decks, went by with hardly a sound as the paddles gently kissed the surface of the water. Peggy waved. She knew them, but then she knew most people on the canal. When she reached Odin and Thor's mooring, the boys and Tim had already left for the cottage. She could see the lights shining beyond the closed curtains and smell the smoke from the burning logs in the fireplace. Barney wasn't waiting for Peggy and stood barking by the front door.

After dinner Peggy watched her EastEnders on her portable television. Tim did not have one, preferring to listen to the radio, so Peggy always had to bring it with her. She was surprised how the boys didn't seem to miss watching television. Zed asked Tim if he could show them how to play chess. They sat quietly whilst he explained the game and identified the names of the different pieces on the board. Barney, having no interest in either television soaps or chess, had fallen asleep in front of the fire. The long day had taken its toll and soon the cottage was in darkness. Only the crackle from the burning logs in the fireplace disturbed the peaceful stillness of that cosy place.

CHAPTER EIGHT

Rose's Secret

Whilst Zed and Dwain were snuggled down in their warm beds at Tim's cottage, Rocket Ron had just returned home to his boat from keeping his vigil at Muckle Farm. It was late, his legs ached and he was tired. From his hiding place in the old barn, he had waited, and waited, listening for the sound of the gate swinging on its rusty hinge, but nothing. This had been the second night that the stranger had failed to show up. He had been tempted to look inside the farmhouse for clues but was afraid the man might return and catch him.

He made a mug of hot tea, threw some coal on the stove, then settled into his old but comfortable armchair. Frankie and Freddie jumped up on his lap to greet him.

'Maybe he's gone, what do you think Frankie?' He always discussed things with Frankie, who was the more sensible, and cleverer of the two ferrets.
Freddie was just a thug, who was always getting into mischief and looking for trouble. Picking Frankie up he stared into his little face. The ferret gave a twitch of his nose.

'I reckon you're right.' Ron said, 'and I doubt we'll ever know what he was up to.' He twitched his nose again, and jumped onto Ron's shoulder. 'Good idea.' said Ron laughing, 'we'll tell Rose tomorrow.' He closed his eyes and fell fast asleep in the chair.

Tim poured himself a strong cup of early morning coffee. Darkness had retreated across the low fields leaving behind a dawn blurred by low cloud and misty rain. He called Barney, took some bread from the cupboard, and walked to the bottom lock gate where Sammy and Sheena would be waiting for their breakfast. He noticed the seepage of water through the gates was getting worse. They would need replacing next winter. Sheena took a piece of bread from Tim's hand. Sammy had climbed out onto the bank and was pulling at the short grass. They would be nesting soon. Of the six cygnets hatched last year only four had survived and these had long since left to find their own mates elsewhere on the canal. The church clock in the village struck seven. Somewhere a cockerel crowed. Further along the towpath the little donkey came to the gate as he always did. Tim fed him a carrot. Barney didn't do carrots. So, he had a dog biscuit.

When he returned to the cottage Peggy told him that Rocket Ron had phoned to say the bloke who had been squatting at the farm had gone.

'How does he know that?'' asked Tim.

'He said there's been no sign of him there for two nights.'

'As I thought.' said Tim, 'a chancer, looking to make a fast buck. Probably been casing the boats on the towpath to see what he can nick.'

Peggy wasn't so sure. 'I still don't like it, seems very suspicious to me, him knowing Zed's name and all that.

Tim shrugged. 'Like I said before, he could have picked up something in the village, you know how people talk.' He poured himself another cup of coffee.

Bleary eyed, Zed and Dwain stumbled into the kitchen.

'Blimey.' laughed Tim, 'you two look like a couple of Zombies.'

'What's the time?' asked Zed scratching his head.

'It's eight o' clock.' replied Peggy, stirring a large pot of porridge.

Zed groaned, 'it's the middle of the night, I'm going back to bed.' Dwain followed yawning.'

'Typical teenagers.' called Tim, as they

94

disappeared back into the bedroom.

Rose stood looking at the naked bear tree. She smiled as, through the cracked and blackened limbs, new green shoots were staring to appear. Soon it would be time to place all the little bears into the burnt willow tree, where at night, when those who had forsaken them slept, they would dance and play in the light of the moon. She knelt and pressed the palm of her hand firmly onto the damp grass.

'Oh dear.' she said loudly, 'your pulse is very weak, what are we doing to you?' Her small wicker basket was overflowing with herbs that she had collected earlier that morning. Only she knew the secret path that led through the woods, and beyond to where the crystal stream ran, and the rich health-giving herbs grew.

She didn't hear Rocket Ron coming. Frankie and Freddie had scampered ahead of him and were sniffing in her basket of herbs. He looked weary. Keeping vigil at Muckle Farm had tired him out. Rose picked up her basket. 'You look in need of a strong cup of tea Ron.'

'I need a strong something.' he laughed.

Ron was very fond of Rose. He would have liked their relationship to have been deeper than just good friends, but he had known since puberty that this wasn't possible. They had known each other a long time and agreed on most things, except food. Rose was a vegan, and Ron could not understand how anybody could survive without eating meat. He rested his weary bones in Rose's rocking chair. 'I came to tell you that the bloke staying at the farm has gone.'

'I do hope so.' she said, looking relieved.

'You still can't think why he was asking about you?' asked Ron.

Rose seemed worried and sat twisting the coloured beads

that she wore around her neck, always a sign that she was feeling anxious. 'I've not been entirely honest with you and Peggy, and I feel dreadful about young Zed being involved.'

'Involved in what?' asked Ron.

'Well, there was a man. Mr Coote employed him for a few weeks, just to tidy up the grounds around the house. But I can't see how he could know, and he seemed such a nice young man.'

'Know what?' asked Ron gently.

Rose sat down opposite Ron.

'As you know, I was the only person that Mr Coote ever saw for nearly twenty years. He said he didn't have any other relatives or friends, and I grew very fond of him, and he of me. I'm not saying there was any.....!' She stopped and laughed, 'well you know what I mean, we were just good friends. Like us.'

Ron smiled.

'He knew he was dying and said he wanted to leave me something to remember him by, and to thank me for my friendship over the years. I said I didn't want anything, but he insisted. A few weeks later he gave me a box, wrapped in gold coloured paper. It was sitting on the coffee table amongst all the old newspapers and magazines that he refused to throw away.'

'Go on then, open it,' he said laughing, "it won't bite.'

'Well, I nearly passed out, it was magnificent.'

Rose stopped talking as a tear trickled from her eye and ran down her wrinkled cheek. 'Magnificent.' she said again, wiping her eye with a tissue.

Ron waited a few minutes, then gently asked Rose what it was. Reaching under the table she pulled out the trunk where all the bears were kept. Opening the lid, she took out Dibble, the oldest of the bears. Sitting him on her lap she took a pair of scissors and cut Dibble open, then reaching inside pulled out a package wrapped in tissue. Rose placed it on the table and gently folded back the tissue paper.

'Oh, my days.' said Ron, not believing his eyes.
Rose lifted it up, a solid gold windlass on a gold chain.

'It must be worth a fortune.' said Ron, still stunned.
She smiled. 'You can see why I nearly passed out, and that wasn't all, he left me his wife's jewellery as well.'

'I didn't know he was married.' said Ron.

'He lost her years ago, it was a sudden illness, I think. He never said much about it. Maybe that was the reason he became a recluse.'

'Were there no other relatives?' asked Ron.
She thought for a moment. 'He did mention a nephew once, but only briefly.'
Ron asked where the rest of the jewellery was.

In the same place.' she chuckled, pointing to the trunk.
Ron was speechless for a moment.

'What if it is the same bloke? if he does know you could be in real danger Rose. Don't you think it would be better in a bank or somewhere secure?'

'I don't trust banks, and who is going to think of looking inside my little bears?'
Ron thought for a moment. 'You'll have to tell Peggy.'

'No', she said firmly. 'It will only worry her, this must stay between us, promise me you won't say anything to anyone Ron.'
He nodded, and reluctantly agreed.
She smiled, 'Good, now how about another cuppa?'

Zed phoned his gran. She asked if he was missing London. He laughed. He asked her if she was missing him. She laughed, and said that it was very quiet without him. His mum had received the postcard that he had sent, and said she was looking forward to seeing him when she is released from prison. He told her that he hadn't heard any more from his uncle Darren. She was pleased at that. The police had raided the flats the other night looking for drugs. Bradley Seaton and his mates had been arrested. Zed thought that was good. He told her about the journey bringing the boats back from Boswell's Yard. She told him that the lift had broken down again. When he told her about meeting Smokey Joe, she asked why he was called Smokey. Zed didn't know, he hadn't thought to ask that. Peggy wanted to speak to gran, so Zed told her he loved her, said goodbye and handed the phone to Peggy.

Zed had a plan. They were sitting on the wooden bench outside the cottage watching as Tim used a kebb, a long rake, to clear a log that had become stuck behind the lock gate.

'What's this plan then?' asked Dwain.

Zed lowered his voice. 'We go to 'Coote's cottage, and see if we can find what that bloke's after.'

'Why should 'e be after anything there?'' asked Dwain.

'It's obvious i'n' it, why else as 'e been 'anging about and asking about Coote's Wood and Rose?'

'What do yer think it is then?' asked Dwain, seeming a little more interested.

'I dunno, could be cash or gold. Old Coote was filthy rich, maybe 'e 'id it under the floor boards, or buried it in the garden.'

'That's stupid.' said Dwain. 'Why would he do that, knowing it would never be found?'

'Maybe 'e told Rose. I don't know, 'e was a bit weird. Still it's worth a look.'

Dwain didn't seem convinced. 'I thought Tim said we

weren't to go in there without him or Peggy.'

Zed laughed, and jumped up. 'E did. You coming or not?'

They crossed over the lock gate where Tim had now cleared the log and was sitting on the balance beam. 'Just going for a walk.' called Zed, as they ran down the bank to the towpath. Barney started to bark. He wasn't happy that he couldn't go with them. It wasn't far to where a tall wooden gate led from the towpath onto the ash track that snaked between the thick trees in Coote's Wood. The boys jumped when a small Muntjac deer dashed from the undergrowth. It was eerily quiet apart from the rustle of the branches in the light wind, and although it was early afternoon the light was struggling to penetrate through the dense overhead foliage.

A small stream followed the course of the path. Zed jumped in and unblocked a dam of broken branches, then watched as the freed water rushed into the gulley. Dwain picked up the remains of a mauled rabbit and threw it at Zed. He speared it on the end of a stick and chased Dwain along the ash path. A hedge of tall conifers ran around the perimeter of the clearing where old Mr Coote's cottage stood. In the small front garden, a sundial rested on a concrete plinth surrounded by bright yellow daffodils.

The whitewashed walls were now dulled and grey. Rotting, blue, wooden window frames held on desperately to their fragile, dirty glass. Fallen roof tiles lay smashed on the concrete path that led to the front door. Zed carefully pushed it open. It led into one large room that smelt of damp. The furniture had been removed, all except an old sofa which sat next to the cold fireplace. Unused logs were still stacked against the wall. The floor was strewn with old newspapers. Zed kicked them to one side and rolled up the soiled rug so he could see the floor underneath.

'What you doing?' asked Dwain.

'Looking for loose floorboards.'

Dwain laughed. 'It wouldn't be that obvious would it?'

'You go and check the kitchen.' said Zed, pressing his foot down hard onto each board.

'What am I supposed to be looking for?

'I don't know, anything out of the ordinary. Use your imagination.'

Zed looked up the chimney, though he wasn't sure why. He ran his hand along the surface of the brick mantelpiece that was covered with thick dust. Dwain opened the cupboards in the kitchen. One fell off the wall and landed with a crash on the work surface. He found a key, and called Zed. It was to the back door. They went into the back garden and searched amongst the long grass for any recently disturbed soil. A fat wood Pidgeon watched them whilst balancing precariously on a swaying washing line.

Dwain opened the door of a rickety wooden shed, but apart from a rusty lawnmower and a few flowerpots it was empty. As Zed lifted a loose paving stone in the path, a disturbed spider shot out and disappeared into the grass. They decided to go back inside and search upstairs. A threadbare carpet covered the creaky steps which led to the two bedrooms and bathroom. Zed checked out the back room. It was bare. A single light bulb hung from the ceiling. He went into the bathroom, lifted the lid on the cistern and looked inside. He'd seen them do this on the television. It's where they always hid a gun or drugs. But it was empty. When he went into the front bedroom Dwain was bouncing on the sprung base of an old metal bed.

'Do yer fink old Coote died on there?' said Zed. Dwain quickly jumped off.

It was Dwain who heard the noise from downstairs.

He poked Zed in the ribs.

'Did you hear that?'

'What?' asked Zed.

'I 'eard a noise.'

They both stood very still.

Suddenly there was a loud bang as the front door slammed, then a rustling noise as the old newspapers were kicked about the floor.

'Who do you fink it is?' whispered Zed.

'Dunno, but we gotta get out of 'ere.' said Dwain. They thought of jumping from the window but it was too high.

'We're trapped.' whispered Zed.

Dwain put his hand over Zed's mouth. 'Just keep quiet, he might go away.'

Then they heard the creak of footsteps of the stairs.

Zed grabbed Dwain's arm, 'he's coming up 'ere.'

'Quick under the bed.' said Dwain, his bladder about to explode.

The sound was low at first, a man's voice, deep and melancholy, becoming louder with each upward step on the stairs.

'Who's in my house?', 'Who's in my house?', 'Who's in my house?'

'Oh god.' cried Zed, 'it's old Coote, 'e's come back from the dead.'

The boys held their breath, clutching tight to each other as the footsteps came closer to the door. The voice roared again. 'Who's in my house?' Then the door flew open. The boys screamed. 'We're sorry Mr Coote.' shouted Zed, 'we didn't mean to……………'

The tall, bearded figure in a long, brown coat stood in the doorway roaring with laughter, the more the boys screamed the more he laughed.

'Smokey.' shouted Dwain, 'you, you frightened the

crap out of us.'

Zed was nearly in tears, 'we thought you were old Coote's ghost.'

Smokey was laughing so much he could hardly talk. 'Your faces were a picture of pure fear.'

"Ow, 'ow, did you know we were in 'ere?' asked Dwain, still fighting for breath.

'I was in the woods hunting rabbits, when I saw you arrive.'

Downstairs, Smokey asked them why they were there.

Zed explained that they were looking for old Mr Coote's treasure.

Smokey smiled. 'I think if there was any treasure here, it would have been found by now.' They walked with Smokey back along the ash path where the gate onto the towpath was.

'You won't tell Tim or Peggy we were 'ere will you?' Zed asked Smokey.

'Your secret's safe with me, us free souls must stick together.' he said patting Zed on the head. They waved as Smokey walked off in the direction of Old Mill Lock.

'What's 'e mean free souls?' asked Dwain.

'Dunno.' replied Zed, 'but I like the idea of it.'

When they got back home Peggy asked them where they had been.

'Just walking about.' said Zed, grinning at Dwain.

'More like getting into mischief.' shouted Tim from the kitchen.

'Well you can walk some more tomorrow.' said Peggy, 'Rose has got some herbal tea for me. She'll be home after four, and this time take Barney with you. He's been looking for you all afternoon.'

An expectant Barney sat looking at them, his ball clutched between his paws.

'Come on then Barney.' called Zed, 'fetch yer ball.' They ran outside.

Dwain threw the ball which bounced off the grass and fell into the lock.

'Very clever.' said Zed. Barney stood on the edge of the lock chamber looking down and whining.

''Ang on Barney, I'll go and get it.' said Zed.

He climbed down the metal ladder that was attached to the inside of the empty lock. The ball was just floating out of his reach. Letting go of the ladder with one hand he reached out, then his foot slipped off the wet rung and he fell with a loud splash into the cold water. Dwain was laughing, Barney was barking.

'Ah, it's freezing.' he shouted, bobbing up and swimming towards the ladder.

'Don't forget the ball.' laughed Dwain.

B....... the ball!' called Zed, as he hauled himself up the slippery ladder.

He ran dripping across the grass to the cottage. Peggy shrieked.

'What on earth have you been doing?'

Zed stood shivering by the front door, a puddle forming at his feet. 'I fell in the lock.'

'He was trying to get Barney's ball.' added Dwain.

Peggy shook her head in disbelief. 'Get those clothes off there, you're not coming in here dripping like that. Then get in the shower.'

Hearing the commotion Tim looked round the kitchen door. He laughed. 'Cold was it?'

CHAPTER NINE

The fox strikes

Darren unhitched his rusty van from the small caravan that he shared with Lee. Their hands were still blotched with yellow paint from painting the upright poles that supported the circus big top. They wouldn't take the train to Melbury today, as the plan demanded a quick getaway, and zero recognition. Lee was nervous, what if the woman they knew as Rose wouldn't reveal where the gear was stashed? He knew Darren could be aggressive and unpredictable and worried what he might do.

Darren jumped in behind the van's steering wheel, threw a bag on the passenger seat next to Lee and turned the ignition key. A huge cloud of black smoke flew from the exhaust pipe as they drove out of the field where De'Vito's circus was resting for the winter. They were heading for a small lane with a lay-by which Darren had located on the far side of Tiddledurn. It was remote and close to the canal. From there they could walk along the towpath towards where Rose's boat was moored.

There would be few people about so they should not be recognised.

Lee looking nervous turned on the radio and rested his feet on the dashboard.

'Yer not getting cold feet on me, are you?' asked Darren.

'No.' said Lee, 'I just want to get it done and get out of there.'

Darren smiled. 'We'll be in and out before you know it.'

'I 'ope so.' replied Lee as he watched the passing countryside unfold out of the window. He had a distinctly uneasy feeling in his stomach as to how this day would end.

Tim scratched his head. 'How the devil did they manage to do this?'

He was standing on the stern of the narrowboat Moorhen. This was one of Harry Martin's hire boat fleet. He looked in disbelief at a very bent and twisted swans neck. This is the curved metal upright section onto which the tiller bar is fitted, enabling the boat to be steered. After receiving Harry's flustered early morning phone call, he had taken the boys with him to the marina to see if he could repair the damage. Harry was in a panic as the boat was due out on hire again the next day. Before they left Peggy had reminded the boys that they had to collect a potion from Rose for her in the afternoon.

She was taking Barney to the vet in Tiddledurn as they thought he might have picked up a tick.

'They say they caught it on the edge of the bridge.' said Harry, 'the boat went through and the tiller bar stayed where it was.'

Tim shook his head. 'They couldn't have been concentrating.' he said.

'Or drunk. 'said Harry, 'I say or drunk.'

'Have you got something these two can be doing while I sort this out?' asked Tim.

Harry thought for a moment. 'I've got just the thing. 'he replied, 'just the thing.'

They walked with Harry back to his office on the other side of the marina.

A wide beam boat had just entered the marina and was mooring next to the diesel pump.

'Go inside boys, I'll be with you shortly, I say I'll be with you shortly.'

Zed pushed open the office door and they both instantly fell in love. Sitting behind the desk was the most beautiful girl they had ever seen. They both stood open mouthed unable to speak. As she stood up, her long brown hair swirled around her shoulders.

'Hello.' she said, 'I'm Kate, Harry's niece, and you must be Zed?' I've heard all about you.'
Zed mumbled something incoherent. Dwain stepped forward and held out his hand,

'I'm Dwain, Zed's friend.'

'Nice to meet you both.' she said. 'I'm on Easter holiday from uni. My uncle needed some help with his paperwork.' She laughed, 'he's not very good with computers.'

'Ah, I see you've met Kate.' said Harry, wiping his hands with a rag as he came through the door. 'She's a clever girl, a godsend, sorts out all my silly mistakes.'
The boys were still transfixed with Kate. Harry took the keys of Kingfisher from a box on the wall and threw them to Zed.

'Right young Zed, do you think you can bring her over to the service point for me. I'm told your steering is very good these days. Then you can fill her up with diesel and water.'
Zed caught the keys. 'Wow, yeah course we can, thanks 'Ary.'

Harry caught Dwain glancing in Kate's direction and smiled. 'Don't worry, Kate will still be here when you get back.' 'I think you have a couple of admirers there Kate.' he said after they had left the office.
She laughed, 'a bit young for me I think Uncle.'
All but two of Harry's hire boats were out on hire, they usually were this time of year. Only Kingfisher and Heron were moored alongside the wooden jetty.
The boys stepped onto the stern of Kingfisher.

'That is one fit girl.' said Dwain.

'She was awesome, man.' replied Zed. 'Did you see 'er eyes?'

Dwain laughed. 'I wasn't looking at 'ere eyes man.'

Zed turned the key in the ignition. A low purr came from the engine below.

Zed had forgotten just how quiet Kingfisher's engine is compared to Odin's thumping. Dwain had gone to the bow to untie the line; Zed did the same with the stern line.

'Let go and shove off.' shouted Zed.

'Gone.' called Dwain jumping on.

Zed pushed the throttle forward and Kingfisher moved slowly off the mooring.

He would have to steer past a line of moored boats, then turn sharply into the middle of the marina before heading round the small island, where the swans nested, before heading for the service point. He smiled to himself, remembering that day when he had run away from his uncle at the circus and stowed away on Kingfisher. Now two years later he was being trusted to steer the boat on his own, albeit only for a short distance. He made the sharp turn and they passed close to where Tim was working on Moorhen. He tooted the horn.

'Well look at you.' shouted Tim. 'Well done Zed.'

''Ow's it going?' called Dwain.

'Nearly there.' replied Tim. 'It's as straight as I can get it.'

Zed called to Dwain. 'Ready with the bow line?'

'Ready.' He called back.

Zed dropped the speed, pushed the tiller bar over, and glided Kingfisher onto the service point mooring. Dwain jumped out with the bow line.

Harry had been watching from the window of the office.

'Well done.' young Zed, 'I say well done, not even a bump.'

Zed smiled feeling very pleased with himself. Kate had followed Harry out of the office.

'You'll have to show me how to do that.' she said. Zed blushed. 'Anytime Kate'. he replied smiling. Dwain looked jealous.

It was early afternoon when they left the marina. Harry was pleased that his boat had been repaired and the boys were happy they had met Kate. Barney ran to meet them as he heard Betsy Tim's Land Rover coming down the track. The vet had removed the tick. Tim thought it outrageous when Peggy told him the cost, and said that he was in the wrong business. She laughed and called him tight.

Smokey threw a stone into the water and watched as the ripples fanned out across the canal. He was sitting on the bank next to the small peace garden by the path that led to the Buddhist Temple. He often came here to think and reflect. It was a warm day for the time of year. He folded his long, brown, double breasted coat and placed it on the grass beneath him. Laying down he closed his eyes and surrended himself to the sun's embrace. A kaleidoscope of colours washed through him as stillness gently tamed his troubled mind. There were too many memories, too many faces, from a time, when fearless young men were sacrificed on foreign soil, and for what?

He sat up, took off his boots and socks and dipped his tired feet into the cool water. Across the canal, a carpet of yellow rapeseed stretched to a low hill where a tractor was being chased by a flock of gulls. He smiled as he thought of Zed and Dwain searching Coote's cottage for hidden treasure. They reminded him of how he was at that age. He knew every inch of Coote's house and grounds.

He remembered when the paint was clean and fresh and the gardens were rich in bloom; the smell of freshly cut grass and thick pork strips sizzling on the outdoor range;

adventure stories he was told about living on a game reserve in South Africa. He remembered building bivouacs in the tangled woods and sleeping in them overnight, then cooking breakfast over an open fire, the gentle nights, when the owls called, and badgers played by the light of the moon. How he used to hate going home to Birmingham after the school holidays had finished.

Over lunch Zed and Dwain told Peggy about Kate, Harry's niece.

'You should 'ave seen 'er Peg, she was really fit.'
Tim chuckled. 'Young love, you two were really smitten.'

'She wants me to show 'er 'ow to steer a boat.' said Zed.

'Well you'll have to hurry.' said Tim laughing, 'she's off to Brazil next week.'
The boys looked disappointed.

'Don't worry.' said Peggy, 'there's plenty more fish in the sea.'

'I don't want a fish for a girlfriend.' replied Zed.

The boys and Barney left the cottage at four o clock in the afternoon to walk to Rose's boat. Peggy had asked them to collect some herbal tea that Rose had made for her. She told them not to stop long, and to be back home before it gets dark. They were in no hurry and sauntered slowly along the towpath, occasionally throwing a stick into the canal for Barney to retrieve. They fed the little donkey a carrot and spoke to a woman whose dog only had three legs.

The small abandoned cruiser that they had played on, had gone. Army Jim was now moored where it had been. He was outside his boat chopping up wooden pallets with an axe, to feed a large fire that was burning on the side of the towpath. A long unsheaved knife hung

110

from his belt. Barney cocked his leg up the pile of pallets, then ran off when Army Jim growled at him. The boys nodded and hurried by. Zed was always a bit frightened of him. As they passed, he blew a cloud of smoke from his cigarette in their direction.

The boys recognised the smell from their estate in London. It was no ordinary tobacco.

There was a sudden roar overhead as a giant Hercules aircraft flew in over the canal. They watched as it climbed into the low clouds before disappearing. Neither Zed nor Dwain had ever been on a plane. Zed often watched from the balcony of the flats at home, as the planes descended into docklands City Airport. The boys waved as two narrowboats went by. One had a pair of Jack Russell dogs on the roof. They raced up and down the length of the boat barking at Barney. He ignored the yappy terriers and instead went rooting about in the undergrowth.

Passing the entrance to Harry Martin's marina, where they had been earlier in the day, they were tempted to go in and see if Kate was still there but decided against it as it would make them late back. Barney had run ahead to where two young men were fishing and was helping them demolish a packet of digestive biscuits. They were very friendly and showed the boys the fish they had in their keep nets. One of them offered the boys a can of lager. They refused and said they were only thirteen. The men laughed and said, 'so what.'

The path to Muckle Farm was overgrown. Apart from Rocket Ron there were no regular visitors any more. The boys sat on the bank just below the gate that hangs on the rusty hinge. A floating plastic bottle provided the target for skimming stones. Rose's boat was moored just around the next bend, so they had plenty of time.

Darren turned his old van off the main road and onto the narrow lane that weaved its way between high hedge rows and occasional homesteads. Lee, who had been sleeping since they had left Taunton, woke with a start after Darren suddenly hit the brakes when a tractor pulled out of a farmyard. Darren swore and blew the horn. They followed the slow-moving tractor until they reached the next junction, where the road bridge crossed over the canal. It was a small layby. A mattress and a motorcycle with one-wheel missing had been dumped at one end, next to a pile of gravel. Darren pulled in and parked up. Opening the bag, he pulled out two hoodies.

'Ere put this on.' he said passing one to Lee, 'we don't want 'em seeing your ugly mush.' Talk for yourself.' replied Lee pulling it over his head.

There was a narrow track that led down the bank to the towpath. A cluster of boats was moored by the bridge. From here it was only a short distance to where Rose's boat was moored by the willow trees. They passed a group of red-faced cyclists, and a dog walker, but other than that it was deserted. Lee pointed out Rocket Ron's boat as they went past.

Rose had just finished making Peggy's herbal tea, and was decanting it into a small flask. The boat rocked slightly as someone stepped into the bow well. She didn't hear the first knock and was surprised by the force of the second. Turning the key, she was thrown backwoods as Darren and Lee burst through the door. Rose screamed. Grabbing her by the arm Darren pushed her into the chair next to the fire.

'Right you old bird.' he shouted. 'We 'ain't got time for fun and games, where's the gear?'
Rose was confused. 'What gear?' she asked breathlessly.
Putting his hand round her slim throat he asked the question again loudly.

112

'You know what I'm talking about, the jewellery, and that golden windlass necklace that old Coote gave yer?' Rose shook her head. 'I don't know what.....' Darren tightened his grip, his dirty fingernails pressing into her fair skin.

'Don't even go there, love.
Lee shouted. 'Don't hurt 'er Darren.'

'You shut up and carry on searching.'
Darren took a long piece of cord from his bag and tied Rose tightly to the chair.

'You got one last chance.' he said. Rose's hands and legs were shaking and she could feel the tears welling up in her eyes.

'There's nothing 'ere.' called Lee, pulling the contents of the cupboards and drawers onto the floor.

'There 'as to be.' said Darren. Keep looking.'

Zed checked the time on his phone. 'You better stay 'ere with Barney.' he said to Dwain,'e always chases Rose's cat. I won't be long.' Dwain nodded. 'OK'
He skimmed another stone at the bottle floating in the canal. Barney chased after it and belly flopped into the canal.
Zed rapped on the top of Rose's boat. 'It's Zed, Rose. You there?'

Darren, recognising Zed's voice, put his hand over Rose's mouth, then whispered something in her ear. He gestured to Lee to wait behind the door.
Rose called, 'come in Zed.' As he came through the door Lee grabbed him in a headlock and forced him to the floor.

'Get 'is phone.' shouted Darren. Zed yelled and struggled as Lee knelt on his chest and searched through his pockets. Darren threw Lee some cord from his bag.

'Tie 'is hands behind 'is back, then chuck that

phone in the canal.'

Zed shouted and squirmed, 'Get off me you......, leave me alone.'

'Be quiet, you little turd.' said Darren, 'or you'll get a thump.' Zed could smell the familiar stale tobacco on his breath.

'Is that you Darren?' asked Zed.

'I told yer, keep yer mouth shut.'

He turned back to Rose. 'Last chance lady, don't mess with me,' he said angrily.

Dwain was getting cold. He checked his watch. Nearly an hour had passed.

Zed should have been back by now. He called to Barney and walked along the towpath towards Rose's boat. As he reached the bear tree the door opened, and a man came out and threw something in the canal. Although he was wearing a hoodie Dwain was sure it was the man they had met previously on the towpath.

Dwain quickly grabbed Barney and hid behind a willow tree.

'What's he doing on Rose's boat?' he said to Barney.

He told Barney to stay, then waited until the door had closed behind the man before walking slowly to the boat. Peering through the window he could see Zed sitting on the floor, with his hands tied behind his back. The man who he had just seen, was emptying the contents of a box onto the table. Ducking down he crept along the side of the boat so that he could see through another window. He couldn't make out Rose.

Darren was losing it. Rose's stubborn refusal to tell him the whereabouts of the Golden Windlass was making him even more angry. He screamed in her face, his eyes bulging, before picking up a china bowl from the table and smashing it to pieces on the floor. Rose sobbed.

Frightened, Dwain ran back to Barney and the cover of the willow tree, then rang Peggy's mobile. It was a few minutes before Peggy understood what he was talking about. She told him to go to Rocket Ron's boat and stay there with Barney. She would call PC Thomas in the village. Tim had already jumped into Betsy and was speeding towards Muckle Farm.

Zed swore and kicked out at Darren as he tried to free his hands from the rope. Darren laughed at him and took no notice.

Rose couldn't take anymore' she whimpered, 'I'll tell you where they are.'

'Good girl.' said Darren,

Rose pointed to the trunk containing the bears under the table. 'They're in there.'

Dwain banged on the door of Rocket Ron's boat. Ron listened as Dwain breathlessly told him what was happening in Rose's boat. He picked up a baseball bat that he kept behind the door and called Frankie and Freddie. Dwain said he wasn't going to stay there and wanted to go with him.

Rose cried as Darren took a pair of scissors from the galley and started cutting open the small bears in the trunk. It wasn't long before he discovered what they had come for, an assortment of beautiful and expensive jewellery that once belonged to old Mr Coote's wife. Darren picked up Dibble, the oldest of the bears. He cut along the front of the bear. Putting his hand inside he pulled out a package wrapped in tissue. Laying it on the table he tore it open then lifted it up. It was a solid piece of gold cast in the shape of a windlass. Darren laughed out loud. 'This lot's worth a fortune Lee.'

Lee nodded. 'We need to get out of 'ere quick.'

Zed called Darren a waster and told him he wouldn't get away with it.

Darren chuckled. 'And who is going to stop us, little nephew? You?'

Rocket Ron and Dwain crept quietly towards the stern of Rose's boat.

Ron listened at an open window in the bedroom, as Darren and Lee discussed what to do with Rose and Zed. Ron whispered to Dwain. 'We have to do something. By the time Tim and the Police get here they'll be long gone.' Darren tightened the cord binding Zed and Rose. Rose cried out loudly as the coarse rope chafed her skin.

'Right, that's it.' said Ron angrily. He picked up Freddie and dropped him through the open window. Lee was hurriedly putting the gear into a bag when he felt an excruciating pain down below. He screamed in agony as Freddie bit hard into his crutch. 'Ah, ah! Get it off.' he shouted, running around the boat with Freddie swaying from side to side. But Freddie hung on sinking his teeth in even deeper. Darren grabbed a frying pan from the galley and was about to take a swing at Freddie when the front door burst open and Barney raced into the boat. Jumping up he locked his powerful jaws around Darren's wrist. Rocket Ron followed behind and with one heavy swing of his baseball bat knocked Darren out cold. Barney laid across him on the floor holding tight to his wrist. Lee was yelling and doubled up in pain. He was offering no resistance.

Rocket Ron pulled Freddie off, and stood over Lee with the baseball bat.

'Am I glad to see you!' said Zed, as Dwain undid the cord from him and Rose.

Ron passed the baseball bat to Dwain, then pulled the hoodie back from Lee's face.

'Is this the bloke you saw on the towpath? he called to Zed.

Zed nodded. 'Yeah, and the other one's me uncle.'

116

'Watch him Dwain.' said Ron, 'while I see to Rose, if he so much as moves, belt him.'

'No probs.' said Dwain grinning.

Poor Rose was in a terrible state of shock. Ron put a blanket round her and gave her a big hug. Tim screeched to a halt at Muckle Farm. Two police cars with flashing blue lights followed him into the yard. Tim hadn't run for a long time and was soon overtaken on the towpath by the younger and fitter police officers. PC Thomas was first through the door of the boat, though it wasn't as he expected. Darren was just coming around, though his hands and feet had been tied tightly with cord. Lee was still sitting on the floor holding his crutch and whimpering. PC Thomas looked shocked.

'How did you............?   Ron interrupted him. 'Surprising what a dog and a ferret can do.' he laughed.

Tim came through the door. 'Are you all ok?' he said, fighting to get his breath.

'We are.' chuckled Zed, 'but I don't know about them.'

PC Thomas and his colleagues handcuffed Darren and Lee and took them back to their police cars at Muckle Farm.

Rose stayed with Tim and Peggy at the cottage for a week while she recovered from her horrible ordeal. All the little bears and their contents went with her. Ron and Tim repaired the damage to her boat and Peggy and the boys cleared up the mess inside. Peggy and Rocket Ron insisted that Rose put the golden windlass and the jewellery somewhere secure. She agreed and put it in a safe deposit box at the bank.

Peggy took the boys to Melbury so she could buy Zed a new phone. Zed phoned Gran that night and told her what had happened. She cried and said she was pleased they were alright and that she never wanted to see or hear from Darren again. Barney got a large pig's ear as a treat, and Frankie and Freddie, two freshly killed juicy rats, a present from Wills, Jean's tom cat.

CHAPTER TEN

Back to the smoke

The last few days of the holiday passed in a quickening blur. Although the boys had put returning to London at the very back of their mind, reality, that bane of childhood would soon interrupt their idyll. After breakfast on their last full day, they walked along the towpath to where Odin and Thor where moored. Zed jumped onto the stern of Thor and placed his hand on the tiller bar.

'One day I shall run these two boats.' he said to Dwain. 'I don't want to be
anywhere else, when I leave school. This is where I shall live.'

''Ave yer spoken to Tim yet about teaching yer to be a mechanic?' asked Dwain.

'Not yet, but I know 'e will.'
They walked along to say goodbye to Jean. Wills, her fat tomcat, was as usual lying on the wooden bench outside the shop. Dwain bent down to stroke him.

'I wouldn't if yer wanna keep yer fingers.' laughed Zed.

This was the first time that Jean had seen the boys since the incident on Rose's boat.

'You two deserve a medal.' she said.

Zed laughed. 'It wasn't us, Freddie and Barney where the main men.'

Jean gave them both a big hug and a large bar of chocolate each. 'So back to London tomorrow, I hear?' The boys nodded glumly. 'Well you have the Summer holidays to look forward to.' she said. Zed nodded again. Dwain stayed quiet. One of Harry Martin's hire boats had moored at the bottom of the garden and the family were walking up towards the shop. Zed said, 'Hello.' but didn't understand the reply.

'French.' said Dwain.

'Don't think Jean sells frogs' legs.' said Zed, and they both ran laughing along the towpath. Tim was loading his welding equipment into the back of the Land Rover. The boys closed the lock gates after a boat had gone through, then crossed over to the cottage. Tim said he had a job to do at Harry Martin's marina, so they jumped in the back of Betsy and went with him. They were hoping to see Kate, but she had already left for Brazil. Harry offered them some pocket money if they washed down the outside of two of his hire boats. Inevitably, they both ended up wet. Zed pretended that he had lost control of the pressure hose, soaking Dwain. Then a soapy sponge just happened to fly out of Dwain's hand hitting Zed full in the face. Harry was happy with the result though and gave them five pounds each. While Tim was finishing off his welding, they walked Barney around the perimeter of the marina, although by now they were feeling the wind chill through their damp clothes. When they got back to the office Tim and Harry were sitting inside drinking tea.

'Harry's got a proposal for you Zed.' said Tim. Harry explained that he could do with some help at the marina in the summer holidays, and now that Zed was older, would he like to do that? Zed looked at Tim. 'Is that alright?' he asked.

Tim laughed, 'of course it is, get you out of our way for a couple of days.'

Harry and Zed shook hands. 'That's a deal then, I say that's a deal.' said Harry.

'And of course, we'll pay you.'

Driving back Dwain was quiet. 'What's up?' asked Zed.

'Just thinking 'ow lucky you are 'aving all this down 'ere.'

Zed thought for a moment, "S'pose I am, but it was only by chance. What if Peggy 'ad been a different sort of person and called the old bill when she found me on Kingfisher? I might 'av ended up in a children's 'ome.'

They didn't say much else to each other, their thoughts were on tomorrow morning, when reality would come haunting like a bad dream.

That evening they had a fish and chip supper. Peggy had invited Rocket Ron and Rose. Tim had tried tracking down Smokey Joe but he had disappeared somewhere on his travels. The boys would be disappointed, they liked Smokey. Nobody spoke of the incident on Rose's boat. But Rocket Ron did say he had heard that Darren and Lee had been remanded in custody by the magistrate. After dinner Peggy and Rose watched the soaps on television while Tim, Ron, and the boys played chess doubles. Tim and Dwain V Ron and Zed. Ron and Zed won. It was late when Tim left to take Ron and Rose home.

'Yer reckon that bloke really did walk on the moon? 'said Zed looking out of the bedroom window at the night sky, twinkling with stars.

'What bloke?' asked Dwain sleepily.

Zed shrugged. 'I dunno 'is name, it was a long time ago.'

'Don't see the point.' replied Dwain, rolling over and closing his eyes.

'Well I wouldn't mind going to the moon.' said Zed, climbing into bed, 'it's gotta be better than the dump we live in.' Dwain didn't answer he was already asleep.

Reality swirled in with the cold, grey dawn. Its intrusion expelling the comforting darkness of the warm room. The boys had packed most of their clothes the previous night. Breakfast was eaten without much enthusiasm. 'Right, you ready then?' called Tim from outside the front door. The boys threw their bags into the back of the Land Rover then climbed in next to Barney. Peggy sat next to Tim in the front. Nobody said much on the way to the station in Melbury. Peggy was going to travel with them to Paddington Station where Gran would meet them.

The train was late. Tim grumbled. 'It's always late.' Arriving very slowly it emitted a screeching metal on metal sound as the wheels hugged the bend in the rails before stopping at the platform. Peggy went to find the seats she had reserved, whilst the boys said goodbye to Tim and Barney. Tim put his big thick arms around both their shoulders. 'Now you two behave yourselves and work hard at school. I'll see you in the summer.' Zed bent down and gave Barney a big hug. Barney gave Zed his paw and licked his face. Dwain patted him on the head. Peggy called from further along the train.

'Come on, it's this carriage.' The boys turned to wave, but Tim and Barney had gone.

As the train gathered speed the boys watched from the window as familiar landscapes became unrecognisable, lanes emptied into main roads and motorways, carrying fast moving traffic. Country villages and farms with green fields and hedgerows morphed into grubby industrial estates and large busy towns. The boys tried recognising the signs on the station platforms, but the train was moving too fast. Peggy went to the buffet car and bought some sandwiches and drink. She complained about the prices. The boys closed their eyes and wished that they were travelling in the opposite direction. The train slowed as it reached the outskirts of London and soon the loudspeaker was announcing the imminent arrival at Paddington Station. Stepping from the train on to the platform they were engulfed in a mass of people, all moving in different directions, pushing, shoving, shouting. Zed felt sick. When they eventually arrived at the automatic ticket barrier Gran was waiting to greet them. Zed forced a smile and gave her a hug. Of, course he was pleased to see her, he just didn't want to be back in London. Gran and Peggy kissed.

'Here they both are, safely delivered.' laughed Peggy.

Peggy only had half an hour to wait before her return journey to Melbury. They walked to the platform where her train was due to leave from. Zed could feel the tears welling up in his eyes.

'It's been really nice having you to stay, you must come and see us again.' she said to Dwain kissing him on the cheek. 'Thanks Peggy, I've really enjoyed it.' he replied. Zed fighting back the tears threw his arms around her. Peggy bit her lip hard, gave him a hug and a kiss on the forehead. 'You be a good lad for your gran now, young man.'

Zed nodded and wiped his eyes.

They waved as Peggy disappeared into the milling crowds on platform nine, before heading down into the underground and home to the housing estate in Rotherhithe, South London.

When Zed woke up the next morning he could hear and smell South London. Dwain was calling for him at eight o clock to walk to school. He showered, then dressed in his school uniform and tried to eat some breakfast. He felt like a prisoner. Opening the front door, he went out onto the balcony so he could breathe. A plane was starting its decent into city airport. Zed wondered where it had come from. He heard the lift rattling from side to side in the shaft. It was Dwain. He looked tired and said he hadn't slept last night. Zed kissed his gran goodbye, then they took the lift back down to the ground floor. It smelt as usual of strong disinfectant.

They walked past the George pub at the entrance to the estate. Heavy traffic was pouring off the roundabout and into the mouth of the tunnel that took it under the Thames to East London. Zed could smell the exhaust fumes. He pulled his hood up over his head as a chilly drizzle blew in from the river. Old Dewey, the crossing patrol man, was waiting by the main road, his vivid coat and hat like a splash of yellow against a grey canvas. He always held everybody until there was a big group before he would walk into the road and stop the traffic. The boys chuckled as a fresh dew drop fell from the end of his long nose and landed on the pavement. He wiped his sleeve across his face.

'That's gross.' laughed Zed.

'Right, over you go, you lot.' he shouted holding his lollipop up high.

The kids walked and ran across the road to loud shouts of, 'Cheers Dewey', and 'Snotty Dewey.' He shuffled miserably back to the pavement to await the next group and more insults. There were two parts to the comprehensive school, the main building and the annexe. Now in year nine they were both in the main building.

Their classroom was on the second floor overlooking the car park. Miss Swan, the teacher with the long neck, was waiting by the classroom door. As Zed passed, she touched him on the arm. 'Hello Zed, so what adventures have you been up to on the canals this Easter?' He looked at Dwain and smiled. 'You'll never believe it if I tell yer Miss'.

GLOSSARY OF TERMS

TO GO ASTERN:

To go backwoods on a boat.

AQUEDUCT:

A bridge, usually with several arches, carrying a water-filled channel such as a canal or river, or road, river or valley.

BILGES:

The lowest compartments of the boat, beneath the water line.

BOLLARD:

A post made of wood, iron, or stone on a bank or quay, for mooring a boat to.

BOW:

The front end of the boat, pronounced to rhyme with 'now'.

BOW LINE:

The rope on the front of the boat.

BUCKBY CAN:

A traditional design of water can, often decorated with roses castles, used by families on the old working boats.

BUCKIT & CHUCKIT:

A basic toilet consisting of a small, metal bin (the bucket') with a wooden seat, that would have to be emptied when full (chuckit').

BUOYANCY AID:

A zip-up jacket to keep you afloat in the water.

BUTTY:

A narrowboat without an engine, which is towed by a motor boat with an engine, either alongside or behind.

TO CAST OFF:

To untie the lines from the mooring and get under way.

CHAMBER:

The watertight enclosure between the top and bottom gates of a lock.

CLEAT:

A metal T-shape on the bow of the boat or on a jetty to tie the mooring lines around.

CLUB HAMMER:

A large, heavy hammer used for driving mooring spikes into the ground.

CUT:

Another name for the canal, reflecting the fact that it was 'cut' out of the ground by the Navvies.

FENDERS:

Protective buffers, usually cylinders, made of plastic or rope, these are hung on the side of boats to protect them from damage when banging against lock sides or gates, banks or other boats. Larger fenders of various shapes are hung at the bow or stern of boats to protect them from bumps.

GALLEY:

The name of the kitchen on a boat.

GONGOOZLERS:

A person who idly watches the labour of others while declining to offer assistance or become involved.

GUNWALE:

(Pronounced 'gunnel') The narrow ledge running down the side of the boat along which you can walk from the front (bow) to the back (stern).

GUY STRAPS:

The rubber bands that keep the canvas attached to the cleats.

HATCHES:

Openings in the boat, either hinged vertical doorways in the sides or sliding horizontal hatches in the roof. Can also be used as emergency exits.

HEADS:

The name for the toilets on a boat.

HURRICANE LAMP:

An oil or paraffin lamp with glass sides to prevent the flamefrom being blown out in the wind.

JETTY:

A wooden, metal, or concrete platform that a boat can moor alongside.

LEGGING:

The method of moving horse-drawn, engine-less boats through tunnels by lying on planks across the roof and 'walking' against the sides of the tunnel. The horse would be led over the top of the tunnel to meet the boat on the other side.

LOCKS:

Water-filled chambers with gates which can be opened and closed to let boats through. At either end of the chamber arepaddles which can be opened and closed to let water through to raise and lower water levels in the chamber, enabling boats to be carried between stretches of water of different levels, i.e. when going up and down hills.

TO MOOR:

To stop alongside the canal or river bank or a wharf.

MOORING SPIKES:

Spiked metal stakes which are banged into the canal or river bank with a club hammer, to tie to when mooring.

NAVVIES:

Short for 'navigators', the labourers who dug the canals or 'navigations' using just shovels and pickaxes.

OUTLET:

A place where water runs into the canal from a building or stream.

PADDLE:

A sliding gate which when lifted allows water to either enter the chamber of a lock from the upper pound, raising the level in the chamber, or to flow out of the chamber into the lower pound, lowering the level in the chamber.

POUND:

The level stretch of water between two locks.

PROPELLER:

A revolving shaft with spiral blades that causes a boat to move (i.e. 'propels' it) by spinning round and creating a backwood thrust of water.

ROSES AND CASTLES:

The popular name for the traditional paintwork of narrowboats.

RUDDER:

The means of steering a boat, this is a large vertical pivoting blade mounted under the water at the stern of the boat, controlled by the tiller bar or sometimes by a wheel.

STERN:

The back end of the boat.

STERN GLAND:

The area around the propeller shaft at the point where it exits a boat's hull underwater, and is packed with wadding and grease. This is the most common method of preventing water from entering the hull while still allowing the propeller shaft to turn. The grease is 'topped up' after each journey by turning a screw on a grease-packed piston.

STERN LINE:

The rope at the back or stern of the boat:

TIE OFF:

Secure the boat by its lines to a bollard or cleat:

TILLER:

The brass bar used for steering the boat. To move the boat left, the tiller is moved to the right, and vice versa.

TOWPATH:

The path next to the canal from which horses once towed boats before they had engines.

TOW ROPE:

The rope used to tow the butty along behind the boat with the engine.

VIADUCT:

A bridge usually composed of several small spans, built to carry a road or railway over a valley.

WASH / WAKE:

The v-shaped wave set up by a boat travelling fast, which will rock other boats it passes, particularly in shallow water.

WEED HATCH:

A hatch at the stern of the boat to access the propeller in order to remove weeds and plastic bags which can get wound round it, preventing the propeller from turning.

WHARF:

A landing place or pier where boats can tie up to load or unload.

WINDING HOLE:

A wider area of canal where even the longest boats can turn. Pronounced as in 'the west wind', not 'winding a watch'.

WINDLASS:

Also known as a lock handle or key, this is a metal handle used to wind open the paddles on a lock.

Printed in Great Britain
by Amazon